HELL HOUSE

Returns

Brenda Hampton

Brenda Hampton Entertainment

P.O. Box 773

Bridgeton, MO 63044

To all of my wonderful readers . . .

THANK YOU!

Jada

OMG! I was so glad when I received a call from, Alex, the new producer of Hell House, asking if I wanted to come back and host the new show. Since I was considered the *winner* and everything from last time, I couldn't say no. I wasn't sure who else would return to the house or how many new people would come, but I was all for it. I had been on pins and needles, ever since I got the call. When I told my fake-ass friends about the invitation, I mean the offer, they advised me not to go there again. Why? I didn't know. I didn't have anything to lose, and since me and my cheap boyfriend had gone our separate ways, I was now single again. Plus, Alex said I would be paid ten grand for hosting Hell House. I'd be a fool to turn down that kind of money, especially since the money Jaylin had given me had already run out. I tried to spend it wisely, but I always had an urge to have brand-named stuff and the finer things in life. The good thing was, I had purchased a car; a car that was slightly banged up because I'd gotten in a little accident. The old, gray-haired woman in the other car claimed the accident was my fault, even though she was the one driving slow. She slammed on the brakes, causing me to hit the back of her car so hard that her wig fell off. All I did was bruised my breasts when they'd hit the steering wheel. Sadly, though, I didn't have insurance. My car didn't get fixed, neither did hers. She was in the process of trying to sue me, so I hoped that Jeff would be able to give me the ten grand upfront. I surely needed the money, and I was on my way to Hell House right now to claim it.

The Uber driver had been running her crooked mouth ever since I'd gotten in her car. It was smoky as hell, and I was kind of upset because the smell had drowned out my sweet smelling perfume. I didn't want to return to Hell House looking like crap. There were some nasty things said about me last time, and if any of those fools from before returned, I wanted to show them I had kicked things up a notch. The tight Levi's I wore tucked in the extra weight I'd picked up just fine. My money-green blouse was low-cut and showed a healthy portion of my cleavage that my bra couldn't contain. I sported green contact lenses, MAC eyelashes and my sandy-brown hair was in a bushy ponytail that looked every bit of natural. Thick and sexy defined me, and the glow of my brown skin was simply irresistible. Maybe I would find somebody to hook up with this time; then again, I wasn't really looking for my soulmate in Hell House. All I would get there was a wet ass—I needed more than that for sure. Still, I couldn't help but to wonder what the men would look like this time around. And the last person I wanted to see, again, was Prince. I could deal with Roc again—even with Jaylin. But if Prince showed up, Jeff would have to offer me twenty grand to stay, instead of ten.

"I should be at your destination in about ten more minutes," said the woman driver while looking in the rearview mirror. "This is a long way. I don't ever think I've been to this area before, and the houses are nice. Who do you know over this way? Your man or someone else?"

She had been asking me too many damn questions. When I'd first gotten in the car, she asked how many kids I had. Then she wanted to know if I was married. Now, she's asking about my man. What's next . . . my dog? What about the size of my panties? Did she need to know that too?

"A friend of mine lives out here," I said, rolling my eyes. I didn't care if she saw me or not. It was a hint for her to mind her own business.

"Well, your friend must be filthy rich. What does he or she do for a living?"

I sighed, before getting her in check real quick.

"Look lady. I don't know why you keep asking me questions, but where I'm going, who I'm with and how much

3

money they have really ain't your business. Just take me to my destination and stop trying to be *pacific* about my whereabouts."

Caught off guard by my attitude, she snapped her head to the side, causing the car to swerve. I wobbled around in the back and had to hold on to the seat so I wouldn't hurt myself.

"Will you please turn around and watch where you going? You don't need to turn your head to look at me. The rearview mirror works just fine."

She winced while evil-eyeing me in the rearview mirror.

"Excuse me for asking you too many questions. I was just trying to spark up a conversation so the ride would go by faster. And by the way, I wasn't trying to be specific, not *pacific*, about your whereabouts. You already told me where you were going, so I'm not sure why you're barking at me."

"Dogs bark. Pretty bitches like me clap back. In my dictionary, the word is *pacific*. I'm sticking to it and there you have it."

She shrugged and tightened her lips the rest of the way there. Less than ten minutes later, she parked in front of the house to let me out. I felt slightly bad about my attitude, so after grabbing my luggage from the car, I whispered a soft "thanks."

"Yeah, whatever," she said in a nasty tone. "Have a nice day."

"You do the same, ol' nappy head ho. That's why you got gum in your hair. Good luck on getting it out."

I purposely put the gum in her hair because she had been working my nerves. She sped off, almost knocking me down with her car. I was sure to call and report her later, but for now, it was too early in the morning for me to be ugly. Alex told me to arrive anywhere between nine and ten; it was only 8:55 a.m. I surely didn't want to be late, and with a gray Mercedes parked in the driveway, I assumed he was already here. I strolled my two pieces of luggage up the long driveway, smiling and breathing in fresh air as thoughts of this house brought back so many memories. I wondered how much the inside had changed, and after looking inside of the window, there didn't appear to be many changes, especially pertaining to the contemporary slash modern furniture I saw. I also noticed some of the same colorful artwork on the walls that stretched to the high vaulted ceilings. Seeing the same ol' stuff worried me a bit, because being in one bedroom with other people was a headache for me. Hopefully, I would be allowed to sleep elsewhere, since I was hosting this time.

With my luggage by my side, I reached out to ring the doorbell. Almost immediately, a white guy who resembled Jeff, the previous Hell House producer, opened the door. He was slim, preppy, very attractive with brown hair, and he had a welcoming smile. Kind of reminded me of the New England Patriots' quarterback, Tom Brady, but not quite.

"You must be Jada," he said, widening the door for me to come inside.

"That would be me." I reached for my luggage, but he grabbed both pieces from the porch, bringing them inside.

"I'll take your luggage to the bedroom later, and I'm so glad you're here. We have an enormous amount of things to cover, before the other participants arrive. So follow me and relax."

Alex made his way down the hallway and into the sitting area that was near the opened kitchen. The furniture was different, but the large gray sectional and comfy chairs provided plenty of seating for everyone. The kitchen now had a round glass table with five chairs surrounding it. Cabinets were white with crystal handles. Hardwood floors were a darker wood, and a humongous TV was mounted on a wall-to-wall entertainment center.

"Before you have a seat," Alex said. "Can I get you anything to drink?"

"No, I'm good. I already ate breakfast, and on the drive over here I finished off my orange juice."

"Great. Well, have a seat and allow me to give you more details about the people you're going to meet soon. More so, about why they've agreed to come here."

I placed my Michael Kors purse on the table then sat on the sofa to listen. My lips pursed instantly when Alex removed a manila folder from his briefcase, laying it on the table. The first photo I saw was of Chase. I rolled my eyes, causing Alex to chuckle a bit.

"Yes, I'm well aware of how things ended between the two of you, but Chase agreed to come back here because she said there was some unfinished business she wanted to take care of. We're not exactly sure what that business consists of, but she was just as delighted to get the call from us as you were."

"Well, I was delighted because you mentioned ten thousand dollars. And since we're on the subject, when can I expect to get it? I don't want no tricky shit like the last time. I want my money upfront, if that's at all possible."

"I'm willing to give you five now, five when this is over."

"How about seven now, three later?"

"I'll have to speak to the other—"

I quickly stood and reached for my purse. "You go ahead and talk to whoever you need to about this and let me know what y'all decide. I need seven upfront or else I'm out of here. I almost

7

left here emptyhanded last time. So you can understand why, if I'm investing my time in this, I would want most of my money upfront."

"I do understand, and I don't think that'll be a problem. Just allow me to make a phone call or two, and I'll have an answer for you soon."

"Cool." I sat back down and crossed my legs. My red-bottom shoes were off the hook, and as soon as I got my money, I was going to buy me another pair. "I'll be right here, so go ahead and make those calls. If you need my checking account number to deposit the funds, just let me know."

Alex looked at me as if I had lost my mind, but I wasn't having it. I was tired of folks trying to screw me over and use me all the time. I needed to make sure they paid me for this, especially since I had to deal with Chase's craziness again. Lord knows I didn't want to see that heifer; I was sure she wouldn't be excited to see me either.

Alex walked off to another room. I could hear him talking to someone from a distance. And while he was away, I peeked at the other folders in his briefcase, trying to see who else was coming. I saw a folder with Roc's photo attached to it. Hated he was coming back too—him and me definitely didn't end things on a good note. Two other folders had photos of women I didn't know. They were cute, but they didn't have nothing on me. When I reached for another folder, my eyes damn near broke from the sockets. It was a photo of our new black president. President of the United States! I couldn't believe what I was seeing—there had to be some kind of mistake.

When I heard Alex coming this way again, I quickly shoved the folders back into his briefcase and scooted over. My shocking expression was still there; I was a bit confused by what I'd seen. I figured I'd wait until he told me about the money deal, before I said anything.

"I have good news and a little bad news," he said, sitting on the sofa again.

I sat with my arms crossed, waiting to hear what he was about to tell me. "I'm listening."

"We're willing to give you the seven grand, but it won't be deposited until next week. We just want to make sure you hold up your end of the bargain and you don't bail out on us. Besides, even if we put the funds into your account today or tomorrow, you won't be able to utilize the money because you'll be here. Like the last time, no one will be allowed to leave the premises."

My head started rolling as I spoke. "I don't care about not being able to utilize the money. I just want to make sure it's in my account. I'm going to roll with it this time, but come next week, my money better be in my account. I will be able to have access to my phone and check, right?"

"Yes. You're the only one who will be allowed to have a phone."

That definitely put a smile on my face. Any privileges I had around here would be beneficial to me. Now that we had the money situation clear, I had to ask him about the photo of the president I'd seen on the folder.

"Thanks for letting me keep my phone. I'm sure I'll need it, just in case I have to call my posse on these tricks in here. Meanwhile, while you were in the other room, I took a look at some of the other folders. Why did I see a photo of the president?"

Alex smiled and sat back with his arms crossed over his chest. "Because he'll be here too."

I clenched my chest and widened my eyes even more. "Are you serious? I mean, why would he, of all people, come here?"

"This time around, Hell House is for people who need space, more than anything. People who are dealing with things in their lives or who may need to just step away from their situations and come here to relax. We reached out to the president, and against his advisors' wishes, he thought coming here would be a good idea. In addition to the money we're offering, not many people were willing to say no this time."

"I still don't get why he would want to come here. With the VP now in charge of things, shit could get ugly while he's away from the White House. I'm good with him being here, but if y'all expect me to stand for the anthem when he's in my presence, or just because, that ain't happening. I'm sitting my black ass down."

"Nobody expects you to stand for the anthem and that's definitely your choice. I don't see why you would need to stand—"

"Because we're supposed to show the president some respect, right?" I swallowed, wondering if this was the right move for me or not, especially if I would have to behave better. "In my opinion, all that foolishness that happened last time can't happen with the president being around. I just don't know—"

I paused when I heard a female's voice, asking if anyone was here. Alex stood and so did I, just so we could see who it was. Seconds later, in walked a real pretty bitch that caused me to scan her from head to toe. Her hair was full of loose, long and wavy curls, makeup was flawless and curves were in all the right and wrong places. The super tight jeans she wore showed off her shapely figure, and with red-bottom heels on, too, Alex was drooling. He rushed up to her, extending his hand.

"I recognize you from the photos," he said. "Scorpio Valentino, correct?"

"In the flesh," she said, looking at him with a flirting smile. "I know I'm early, but I asked a friend to drop me off. This was the only time she could do it."

"No problem. I was just speaking to Jada about her duties here. We still have a lot to discuss, so if you wouldn't mind stepping outside by the pool area and having a drink or two until we're done, that would be great."

"I don't mind at all. Take your time and let me know when the two of you are done."

That trick walked off without even looking my way or speaking to me. Nonetheless, I couldn't keep my eyes off of her. I had never seen that kind of beauty up close and personal, other than looking in the mirror at myself. She must've had somebody helping her look that good. I would die for a body like hers, and I just didn't understand what some women did to make their asses look so perfect like that. It wasn't that mine was bad, but in order for it to look that good, I had to straighten and tighten things up with a girdle. I had on one now, and it was cutting the shit out of my upper thighs. She was probably wearing one too, cause ain't no way she had it going on like that without one.

I turned to address Alex, but his lustful eyes were still locked on Miss Valentino who was now outside. I waved my hand in front of his face to get his attention.

"Excuse me, but if you don't mind me asking, what's her story? Who is she and why is she here?"

"I can't say it's for the money, because she's already pretty wealthy. The million-dollar payout we're offering this time is—"

I stepped back and held up my hand. "Hold up and wait one doggone minute. Did you say a million dollars?"

He nodded. "Yes, I did. It's what we're offering the winner this time. Pretty neat, huh?"

"Pretty neat my ass. How y'all gon' give me a lousy ten grand and then offer the winner one-million dollars? Something ain't right about that, and I feel shortchanged. Obviously, I'll have to stay here until all of this shit is over. I probably have to do all the cooking around here too, because by the looks of that chick out there," I nudged my head toward Miss Scorpio. "She don't look like she's done any cooking in her life."

"We would like for you to do most of the cooking, but that was a request from one of the producers. He felt as if you were a wonderful cook last time and the new people would appreciate your services."

"Don't be trying to make me feel good about this. I want more money or I'm checking out of here. You got until tomorrow to get me more money—at least fifty g's. Y'all are so lucky that I'm willing to stay. Money aside, tell me more about the people coming and what I can expect."

"You already know Chase is coming back and the president will be here. Scorpio is already here, and she happens to be the ex-girlfriend of Jaylin Rogers who was here the last time with you. They have two children together, and they had a long relationship, before he remarried. Scorpio was married too, but she's recently divorced."

"Umph. She is definitely Jaylin's type, but then again, what ho ain't? I wish Sylvia was here so she could tell Scorpio all about what happened the last time. Then again, it probably don't matter. Chase ol' desperate self won't like her, and just so you know, when they start going to blows with each other, I will not interfere. I'm not responsible for breaking up fights, am I?"

"No, we don't expect that kind of drama to happen this time. All we want is for everyone to get along. No one will be voted out of the house this time, and on a daily basis, it'll be your responsibility to contact me and tell me who you think should receive the million dollars. You have to keep your opinion to yourself, and the other people can't know how much your decision will count."

I nodded and finally put another smile on my face. Giving me that kind of authority was perfect. I couldn't wait to get the ball rolling now.

"I think I'm going to like this. Now, have a seat and continue to tell me about the rest of the people who'll be coming here."

Alex removed the folders from his briefcase, and one-by-one, he gave me the scoop on a newcomer named Evelyn and a man named Keith. Roc was coming back, too, but according to Alex, many people thought he was dead.

"He's coming back by popular demand. His wife isn't exactly happy about him doing this, especially since they've been living out of the country for a few years. Not many people know he'll be here, and by the time this show airs, or should I say if it airs, he'll be out of the country again."

"If you ask me, he ain't nothing but trouble. Back by popular demand my ass. He's just coming back to see Chase. And with her and his wife, Desa Rae, being half-sisters, he should stay as far away from here as possible. I hope the newcomers ain't no troublemakers. If they are, they'll have to deal with me."

"Yes, they will because I'm going to leave and this place will be all yours, after I share more of the rules and regulations. You'll be like the boss around here, and you're the only person who will have my number to reach out to me."

I loved the idea of that too, but I was no fool. Alex was just saying this stuff to get me to stay. He knew good and doggone well that the president, nor Roc, would ever answer to me. I wasn't sure what was up with this Keith dude, but I suspected that he wasn't going to follow a woman's lead either. Not to mention the women too. I predicted that they would break some of the rules and not listen to me.

"Finish telling me what else you need me to do and then you can go. I will call you tomorrow about my money. I hope after much thought and consideration, what y'all trying to pay me will increase tremendously."

All Alex did was smile. He filled me in on everything else I needed to know, and after chatting for almost another hour, he gathered his things and left. I looked outside at Scorpio who was standing near the pool, speaking to someone with a smile on her face. She was already breaking the rules with that phone. I marched her way to quickly let her know what was up. I would also signal to her that she had a booger in her nose. That's how I fucked with chicks who thought they were too cute.

Jada

While Scorpio was on the phone, I walked up from behind and tapped her shoulder. She swung around—her expression fell flat.

"May I help you?" she asked.

"Alex and I are finished. I need to show you around and make you aware of some of the rules before the others get here. They should be here soon."

She held up one finger. "Give me a minute. I'm taking care of something pertaining to my kids. I'll come inside when I'm done."

I stared at her nose, focusing in hard on it. Even frowned, as I rubbed my own nose and then pointed to hers. "Ugggh, you need to get that," I said. "Something is hanging and it doesn't look right."

She sniffed then shrugged. "I'll be inside soon. Meanwhile, I really need to take care of something in private, if you don't mind."

Since it was something with her kids, I walked off without saying a word. I went back inside, examining the kitchen cabinets to see what kind of food was inside of them. There was a whole lot of cereal and snacks. Can goods were there too, as well as bread and boxes of quick-fix meals. I opened the fridge and it was filled to capacity. I visualized all kinds of dishes I could whip up with the meats in the freezer, and I looked forward to showing everyone how well I could throw down in the kitchen. For our first day here, I removed some frozen chicken wings from the freezer to thaw them. I wasn't sure what I was going to cook with them, but when I saw some fresh string beans, I removed them from the fridge, placing them on the counter. I opened another cabinet, but before I could search inside, I heard someone with a deep voice call my name. I turned around and right before my eyes stood Roc in all of his sweet and sexy Hershey's chocolate. I couldn't believe that a smile was on his face, especially after the way things had ended. More than that, I was shocked that the motherfucker had gotten even finer. A diamond earring was in his ear, his loose Levi's did wonders for his physique and the button-down shirt he rocked appeared melted on his muscles. I could see a wife-beater underneath his shirt, and I was eager for him to take it off, just so I could get a glimpse of the tattoos on his chest and biceps.

"Don't just stand there, Ma," he said with opened arms. "Say something or come give me a hug."

Absence definitely made the heart grow fonder. Maybe he forgot about how upset he was at the *Hell House Reunion Show* that day. He was so upset that he walked out, claiming that he never wanted to see any of our asses again. That was then, this was now. Now, I rushed up to him like Whitney Houston did when Bobby Brown had gotten out of jail. Roc was my Boo! I squeezed him tight, closing my eyes as I felt every single tight muscle in his frame. Not only that, but he smelled good too. I pressed my coochie as close to him as I could, just so I could feel his meat that I had previously witnessed with my own eyes. He stumbled back, trying to keep his balance as I attempted to wrap my legs around him too. The thoughts in my head were downright nasty. I couldn't help but to think what a fool Desa Rae was for allowing him to come here again. She must've been one confident chick.

"Damn, Ma," Roc said. "It's like that?"

He hugged me tight, as if he'd missed the hell out of me. But when Scorpio came inside, he turned his head to look at her. His arms eased away from my waist; his head was cocked back.

"Damn. I mean, what's up? Who are you?" he asked.

"Scorpio Valentino," she said with a wide smile. "And you are?"

"Roc Dawson." Roc stepped away from me, extending his hand to hers. "What's up? Nice to meet you."

"Same here," she flirted. "I almost hate to admit this, but now I'm glad I came."

His ol' black ass was grinning from ear-to-ear, showing those pearly whites. I hope this wasn't going to be a repeat of last time, when he screwed Chase's brains out in the living room. Roc must've learned his lesson, but from the way he was checking out Scorpio, I wasn't so sure.

"Uh, before you start pulling your dick out and throwing it on the table," I said to him. "Scorpio is Jaylin's ex. You do remember Jaylin, don't you?"

Roc nodded and touched the hair on his chin while still gazing at her lustfully. "Yeah, uh, I do remember him. We holla at each other from time-to-time, but he never mentioned her to me. I need to call and tell that nigga he got very good . . . damn good taste in women."

Scorpio blushed then shifted her eyes to me. "Just so you know, I'm more than just Jaylin's ex. And as we all get a chance to know more about each other, you'll see that referring to me as *only* his ex is not only small, but petty."

I shrugged my shoulders, slightly irritated by her snobby tone.

"I hope you are more than just his ex, but I only mentioned that because Roc knew Jaylin from last time. You can fill me in later on all that other good stuff or fluff about you, but for now, I'm supposed to be showing you around and telling you where you need to put your things. I assume your luggage is still near the front door, right?"

"Yes, it is. I'll go grab my things and then you can give me a tour of the house."

Roc quickly spoke up. "I'll go get your luggage for you. That way, you won't break your long nails."

He winked at her. She laughed, I didn't. My eyes were focused on Roc's wedding ring, and before he stepped away from us, I grabbed his arm.

"I think she can handle getting her luggage, okay? Besides, you and me got some real quick catching up to do. I need to tell you something in private too."

"I can take a hint," Scorpio said. "I can also go get my own luggage, but thanks, Roc. Your kindness is much appreciated."

That hungry glare in her eyes made me sick to my stomach. And when she walked away, you'd better believe Roc had undressed her already and slipped his dick into her muffin. I shook my head and tugged at his arm to get his attention.

"That's a damn shame," I said as he looked at me.

"Wha . . . What's a shame?"

"You. That's who. Why you always looking and acting so thirsty like that, especially when you have a beautiful woman at home? I thought you were soooo in love with Desa Rae. But from how you acting, I can't tell."

"I am and will always be in love with her. I'm just messing around, that's all. You know how I like to flirt, but I promise you it won't go no further than that. So chill, Ma, and stop sweating me already."

"I ain't sweating you. But if you remember, that's what you said last time. And when you present yourself to a woman like that, you make her coochie react. You don't want that to happen, and I don't know if you can control yourself, especially in here."

Roc sighed and stepped a few inches away from me.

"The bottom line is I like to have fun and that's what I came here to do. You gotta have a little faith in me this time, even though some unfortunate things happened last time. I'm a different man. I got mad love for the woman I got at home, but a fine-ass chick like that will get a reaction from me, no doubt. Seeing you caused me to react too. I walked in here like . . . daaaamn, who is that?"

I blushed and playfully slapped Roc's arm.

"You always trying to make somebody feel good. I'm warning you boy. You'd better stop saying things like that. Somebody in here may hurt you, including me."

Roc looked at me with a straight face.

"Hurt me, please. I'm down, if you are, but since I know you a shit talker, and a tease, sex between us will never happen."

"Never say never," I said. If I wanted it to *really* happen, it would. "Just like you never said I would lose any weight. I took the advice I got last time and got my weight together. I'm down every bit of two pounds. Can't you tell?"

Roc lifted my hands above my head, twirling me around.

"Two pounds, huh," he said, examining me. "I can't really tell, but you reppin' that thickness like a mutha."

I spun around like a beautiful ballerina, but unfortunately for me, my feet got tangled and I almost fell on my ass. Thank God Roc was there to catch me. He held me up by my waist, telling me to be careful.

"You be careful too," I said, gazing into his eyes as Scorpio came back into the room. She cleared her throat, causing Roc to divert his attention back to her ol' ugly self.

"I don't mean to interrupt the party, but are you ready to show me around?" she asked.

23

"Yes, I am. As soon as Roc stop being playful, I'll hook you up."

I had to let her know that he was only joking with her, just in case she got her hopes up. I also wanted her to see that he and I had a connection too.

"Go handle that tour," he said. "Then you and me can go somewhere and light that fire, if you know what I mean. I brought plenty of *that* shit with me. Just say the word when you ready to get hooked up."

I knew he was talking about smoking weed, so I had to hurry up and do my thing with Scorpio. She had a slight frown on her face when I headed her way, and the second we entered the bedroom her frown deepened.

"What is this?" she asked, looking around. "Are all of us supposed to sleep in here? I thought the women would have a room of our own. With three beds against this wall, and three on the other wall, I guess we're supposed to all share one room."

"That would be correct. I'm the only one who can sleep in the basement. Alex said there's a room for me down there, if I don't want to sleep in here. As for you, you have to sleep in here. It's not as bad as you think, and we had a lot of fun in this room. I'm surprised Jaylin didn't tell you about it. He likes closets and I bet the closet over there still got his scent inside of it."

I walked over to the closet; Scorpio followed with her arms crossed.

"Since you're so eager for me to see the closet, I guess you must've done something in here with him, right?"

I put my hand on my hip, elaborating and exaggerating a little just to fuck with her, especially since she thought she was the bomb. She kept tossing her long hair back and batting her long lashes.

"Honey, no, I don't get down like that with men like Jaylin. Even though he tried to go there with me, he failed miserably. He did, however, make some progress with a chick named Sylvia. They were in here allllll night one time, and none of us were able to get any sleep. I don't know what he was doing to her, but she was hollering, screaming and moaning at the top of her lungs. She couldn't walk for two days after that, and when I saw him naked in bed one night, I discovered why. He is hooked up right, ain't he?"

Scorpio sucked her teeth. The irritated look on her face said it all. She was upset for sure.

"Is this the only closet where I can hang my clothes? I can't believe this is the only closet around here. This has to be the smallest walk-in closet I have ever seen, and mine at home is ten times the size of this."

Was she trying to brag? I hoped not, because my closet had it going on too.

"It is the only closet, unless you want to hang your clothes in the bathroom. There's only one of those, too, so if you're used to having two or three bathrooms, you can forget it."

"I'm used to having seven-and-a-half bathrooms, but I guess I don't have a choice."

I pursed my lips, watching as she removed some of her fine pieces of clothing, hanging them in the closet.

"You can do that later. For now, let me finish showing you around, before the others get here."

Scorpio hung up one more shirt, before she stepped out of the closet, following me around the house. I showed her where the only bathroom was, took her outside to the pool area where there was also a basketball court, a sandy area to play volleyball, a workout room, and a game room. A sauna had been added and right behind the bar area was a theater room. Hell House had been hooked up even more. I was pleased to see more chilling areas, even though the large pool area with plenty of lounging chairs was enough.

"This will work," Scorpio said as we headed back inside where Roc was. He was chilling back on the sofa with his feet propped on the table. The TV was on and his cell phone was up to his ear.

"Yeah, man, can you believe that shit? That nigga didn't even see it coming. He lucky I'm still on the low right now. Handle that for me, but don't call my house with no bullshit. You already know Desa Rae ain't going for it."

I cleared my throat to get Roc's attention. He looked at me then removed the phone away from his ear.

"What's up?" he asked.

"I hate to break the bad news to you, but you know we can't use phones in here. You got five minutes to hand it over, so if I was you, I'd be calling Desa Rae to say . . . see you whenever."

"I already called her, but gimmie another minute or two. I know the rules, and I promise you'll have my phone in about five minutes."

I was surprised when Scorpio reached out to give her phone to me.

"This isn't my actual phone, but it is the one that I brought here for emergency usage. For now, you can keep it."

I looked around for the bag Alex gave me to put the phones in. He was stopping by tomorrow to pick them up. I expected for him to have an answer about my extra paper. If he didn't, I was leaving.

Just as I dropped Scorpio's phone in the bag I'd placed on the island, I heard heels clacking on the hardwood floors. I looked up and there stood Chase, carrying Louis Vuitton luggage in her hand. There was no smile on her face, and her eyes shifted from Roc, to Scorpio, to me.

"I guess I don't have to ask where I need to take my luggage," she said.

No hello, no what's up, no nothing.

"No need to ask because you already know," I replied with sass in my voice.

To my surprise, Roc stood and offered his help. "You can drop your luggage right there. I'll take them to the bedroom for you. It's the least I can do."

Chase appeared shocked by his kindness too. She dropped her luggage on the floor, walking away. As she headed my way, Roc picked up her luggage and carried them toward the bedroom. She glanced at his backside and rolled her eyes. Even rolled them at Scorpio, before displaying a fake smile that made her makeup crack. Chase was cute, but the makeup she wore was too heavy. The red lipstick was loud and it didn't go well with caramel colored skin. To me, I felt as if somebody needed to pull a casket next to her and park it. She looked dead, and shame on her for letting somebody fuck up her face like that. The only thing she

28

had going for her was her shapely figure that was noticeable in the sweat suit she wore. Her wrapped hair was parted through the middle and hanging on her shoulders. Her hair made up for the horrible makeup, and when I got a chance, I planned to tell her the truth about how awful it looked.

"Jada, to prevent us from getting off on the wrong foot, I just want to apologize for how things turned out last time. It was crazy around here, but this is a new day. I hope you're not still holding any grudges against me, especially since you can be a little petty at times."

I wasn't sure how to take her comment, and only because she apologized, I threw my hand back at her, pretending as if everything was all good, even though I *still* didn't like her.

"Girl, please. I'm over it. This is a new day, and I'm here to do what the producers asked me to do. That's to be your host and run things around here. So chill and have a good time. This here is Scorpio. She's *one* of Jaylin's exes."

I remembered how Chase chased Jaylin, wanting him to screw her so badly. Then again, I couldn't even remember if the two of them had had sex. If they had, I was sure she would let Scorpio know all about it. That was why I mentioned, again, that she was one of his exes.

"You really need to chill with that ex thingy, Jada," Scorpio said. "It's getting kind of old already. Just refer to me as Scorpio Valentino, the newbie in here, okay?"

"Again, I had to mention Jaylin because Chase, well, I'll let her tell you how well she knew him."

Obviously, Scorpio didn't want to hear it. She walked off and didn't even bother to look at Roc as she breezed by him.

"What y'all done started now?" he asked. "Jada, I know you ain't causing trouble already, are you?"

"I didn't do or say anything. Neither did Chase, so get the facts before you start making *acquisitions*."

Chase looked at me, shaking her head. "Girl, you need to work some more on your vocabulary. It's accusations, not acquisitions."

I snapped back at Chase and tightened my fist, just in case she decided to get smart.

"Chase, let me warn you about correcting me. I know what the word is, and I know exactly how it's used. We gon' have a long and terrible time here, if you start going there, okay?"

She zipped her lips and looked at Roc who stood right next to us.

"Thanks for taking my things to the bedroom," she said in a pleasant voice. "And you know I have to ask you this—how is my sister doing?"

"She's doing good. All good, and she told me to tell you hello. She still a little salty about you not staying in touch with her, but I understand why you chose to keep your distance. I'm fine with your decision, because I never thought it would be wise for us to keep in contact with each other."

"Yeah, well, I thought it would be best for all of us, considering what happened between you and me. And just so you know, I'm over it. She made a decision to marry you, and I guess that's a good thing. I surely didn't think I would see you here again, and I'm actually surprised that you came, considering how upset she was about us having sex."

"Roc is back by popular demand," I said, trying to let her know why he was here. "Plus, a million dollars is enough to wake anybody the fuck up, including you."

"Hello?" Chase said, giving me a high-five. "All I want to know is how the winner will be decided this time. I guess someone will tell us soon."

"Hopefully so," Roc said. "The money was a factor, but I'm here because I wanted to be here. I don't have to stay underneath

Desa Rae all the time. When all is said and done, she knows who I'm coming home to."

Roc was so full of shit to me. He was the kind of man who always said one thing and did another. Of course his ass was going home. Home with what . . . a damn disease? I wasn't going to go into details with him or Chase about how to win the money. I damn sure wasn't going to vote for either of them. Well, Roc, maybe.

"Who else is supposed to come?" Chase asked. "Will Jaylin be here too? I hope so. That was another reason why I chose to come back."

"Well, sorry to break the bad news to you, but he won't be back this time. A little birdie told me that he got married again. I think it was to the same chick he was married to before, and she was like . . . you'd better not take yo ass back there to that house."

Chase laughed, knowing damn well that if Jaylin wanted to be here he would. All of our heads turned, however, when Scorpio exited the bedroom in a white bikini that barely covered her goodies. A towel was thrown over her shoulder and dark shades covered her eyes. She paraded by us with her head held high and a smirk on her face.

"I'm going for a swim," she said. "I'm not sure who else we're waiting on, but if anyone needs me, I'll be outside enjoying the beautiful weather."

Neither of us could prevent ourselves from looking at her ass as she made her way to the sliding doors. That bitch's body would put every Victoria Secret's model out of business. With a red rose tattooed on her ass cheek, she knew we would look. Especially Roc who stood with his mouth hanging open, showing how thirsty he was again.

"In about another year or two, hopefully sooner," I said. "That rose on her ass is going to wilt and start to show wrinkles. I hate a trick who acts like her shit don't stink. She need to go sit down somewhere, and ain't no need to be parading around like that in front of married men."

Roc rubbed the tips of his fingers along his goatee. "Trust me when I say us married men appreciate looking at roses like that. Look, I said, but never touch."

Chase and I rolled our eyes at him. I didn't have a good feeling about this, and unfortunately, I was going to have to call Desa Rae up in here to get control of her husband. Roc didn't know I'd had her phone number.

As we stood near the island, talking and laughing about old times, in walked two more people. They were newbies as well, and they appeared to know each other because they were giggling and standing close.

"Hi," the light-skinned chick said, waving. "Sorry I'm a little late, but traffic on Highway 40 is backed up."

"Yeah, the cab I was in got caught up too," the brotha said. "Nonetheless, I made it."

They came up to us, introducing themselves. The chick's name was Evelyn, and the tall, rich chocolate and handsome brotha was Keith. I thought Roc was dark, but Keith was a rich, dark and smooth chocolate. Since I no longer had feelings for Roc's trifling self, my feelings converted to Keith. All this precious chocolate was going to get me in trouble, and why in the hell did the men have to be so sexy? Keith's light brown eyes were everything. I loved a man with narrow and mysterious eyes. He was real buffed—even more than Roc was. And his masculine, baritone voice had my heart racing faster, every time he'd said something.

As for Evelyn, Chase and Scorpio, they were all very decent-looking women, but I didn't appreciate how some lighter skin chicks always felt as if they were special. I was willing to give these ho's the benefit of the doubt. Evelyn barely had on any makeup. Her round face displayed high cheekbones and lips that looked a little injected for puffiness. Her hair was cropped underneath her ears, and with bangs resting on her forehead, I gave her a seven, on a scale from one-to-ten. Her breasts looked fake, and underneath the tight tank shirt she wore, they appeared real firm. Roc had been checking her out too, and from the way she looked at him, I could tell there would be some sex happening in here, possibly tonight. The look in Evelyn's eyes implied that she wasn't the kind of woman who would wait.

"Thanks for offering to take my luggage into the bedroom," Evelyn said to Roc. He had already jumped on it. I guess he was trying to be nice. "If you want me to repay you at any time, you know I will."

Roc smiled—I got sick of looking at his big white teeth. He nodded at Evelyn and walked off with her luggage. Thoughts in her big head swarmed around, and she didn't take her eyes off of him, until he disappeared in the bedroom.

"Wow," she said, looking at me and Chase. "I hope like hell that he's not happily married. Anybody have the scoop yet?"

Chase spoke up before I did. "Yes, he is happily married. Married to my sister and he's only here for fun. The same fun I hope Keith may be interested in. I don't see a ring on your finger, so I assume you're not married. Are you?"

This time, Evelyn replied to Chase. "Not married, but in love with my best friend, Trina. He's here because they needed some space and time to figure out what the two of them really want."

Keith cleared his throat. "Thanks for speaking up for me, but I do have a mouth. No, I'm not married, and the one person I'm deeply in love with is my child."

Well, he cleared that up. Chase was all smiles, but Evelyn was frowning. I wasn't sure why, but I was sure to find out more later.

"What's for lunch?" Roc shouted as he came from the bedroom. He walked toward us, rubbing his hands together. "I know you got something delicious planned for us, Jada. I see that chicken on the counter thawing, but I need something good to eat right now."

From the corner of my eye, I saw Evelyn signal by scratching her cookies. *Did she really just go there or was I tripping?* She did something because Roc's eyes shifted to her, and his smile got wider. I swear I wanted to punch him in his face! If he smiled one more time, I was going to do it and pick up the pieces later.

"I'm not sure what I'ma fix for lunch, but before we eat, I need to show the newbies around. Follow me, and Keith you can bring your luggage too."

We took two steps forward, before Scorpio rushed inside, jumping up and down. Her titties damn near popped out of the skimpy bikini she had on, and her wavy hair bounced up and down.

"I'm sorry, but I have to go pee. Is anyone in the bathroom now?" she asked.

All eyes were on her again. This time, though, Keith spoke up. He was real polite. "I don't think anyone is in there, but would you like some help?"

Scorpio removed the sunglasses from her eyes, placing the glasses on her head. She checked him out; the grin on her face implied she had given his suggestion some thought.

"No, I think I can handle it. But thanks for asking."

She rushed off to the bathroom, ass jiggling all over the place. Roc and Keith looked at each other, bonding real quick as they must've read each other's minds. They gave each other dap without saying a word.

On the other hand, the ladies felt as if Scorpio needed to go put some more clothes on. They didn't have to say anything . . . I could tell what they were thinking. I was seconds away from saying something to her, especially when she came out of the bathroom shaking her wet hands.

"Are there any towels or paper towels around here?" she asked while looking at me. "I didn't see anything to dry my hands with in the bathroom."

I was in complete, utter shock with that nigga Roc removed his shirt and reached out to give it to her. He just wanted his muscles to show—the wife-beater he had on turned the attention to him.

"Use this, Ma," he said to Scorpio. "At least, until we can figure out where the towels are around here."

I was done with Roc. Flirting was cool, but this was too much. He was lucky I couldn't throw his ass out of here right now. If I could, I would. Scorpio had the audacity to take his shirt and wipe her hands with it. She tossed it back to him, and right when she thanked him, three men in suits came rushing inside, as if they were Five-0. They were white men, wearing dark shades with mean mugs on their faces. I assumed they were there for Roc's ass, so I pointed to him.

"There he is," I said. "Rocky Dawson is the one y'all looking for, right?"

His face twisted, brows were scrunched inward. "Looking for me for what?"

"We just need a few minutes to check out a few things," one man said. "Particularly, to make sure there are no major weapons inside."

It didn't even dawn on me that the men were secret service. Nobody knew that the president was coming here but me, so everyone stood in shock as the men rushed around with some kind of detectors in their hands, checking things out.

"Did they do this the last time you all were here," Evelyn said, whispering to me and Chase.

"I don't think so," Chase replied. "But I guess they want to make sure we don't kill each other up in here."

"This is a bit much," Keith replied with a frown on his face. "Especially, since we were already told not to bring any weapons here. Are they saying they don't trust us?"

"Apparently not," Roc added. "This is bullshit. Ain't no need to come up in here, treating us like criminals."

Roc needed to hush. He was going to bring unnecessary attention to himself and so was Keith. I wanted to tell them about the president, but I also wanted it to be a surprise.

"They should be done soon. This is only for our protection," I said, trying to calm everyone down. "We don't know who could have brought what up in here. As heated as things got last time, they just didn't know what to expect from us."

Scorpio flaunted herself over to the sofa and sat down. Evelyn followed, sticking out her breasts, holding in her flat stomach and walking on her tiptoes like she was so cute. These ho's were killing me. Chase took a seat too. Roc and Keith, however, stood with aggression on their faces. They watched the men move around the house, and after they were done, one of the men stood near the kitchen with a walkie-talkie near his mouth.

"All clear," he said.

What seemed like seconds later, in walked the President of the United States. I gasped to catch my breath, wanted to tickle my pearl that had started to throb. Everyone looked at the president as if they were creating a mannequin challenge.

"Take my belongings to the bedroom," the president ordered, speaking to a black man who was carrying several pieces of luggage in his hands.

"Will do, sir. Anywhere in particular?"

"Wherever there is room."

His demanding voice sent chills up my spine. I had seen him on television a-million-and-one times before, but seeing him in the flesh just did something to me. He added more chocolate to the mix, and the tailored blue suit he rocked fit his tight frame to a capital T. The waves in his neatly lined hair flowed, and with a cleanly shaven face, I had forgotten all about Roc and what's his face. I looked at the flag pin on his lapel, happily stood, placed my hand on my chest that was beating real fast and started singing the anthem.

"Ohhhh say can you seeeee, by the dawn's early light. What . . . We so proudly we give, by the twilights last gleaming. And the rocket's red glare, the bombs busting in air, gave proof through the niiiight, that a flag was still there. Ohhh say does the star spangled banner yet waaaave. For the land of the freeeeeee and the home of the braaaave."

Everybody, including the president, looked at me like I had lost my mind.

Scorpio

I sat in awe, looking at Jada as she attempted to sing the National Anthem after the president had entered the room. I wasn't sure why she insisted on making a fool of herself, but I was relieved when she was finished and had taken a seat where she belonged. The president ignored her foolishness, as he should have. He politely spoke to everyone, before going back outside with the man he'd walked in here with. After he left, we all turned to Jada for answers.

"Is he really staying here with us?" Chase asked with wide eyes. "I can't believe this, oh my God."

Jada's head nodded like a bobble-head doll. "Yep. He's our special guest, so y'all better have y'all act together. Let's all try to get along this time, and if anybody got a beef with anyone else in here, speak now or forever hold your peace."

I gave Chase a slight glance, but I kept my thoughts to myself. I didn't necessarily appreciate the way she had spoken about Jaylin, and the way Jada kept bringing him up was rather disrespectful to me too. I was here to forget all about Jaylin. He and Nokea were married again—so be it. I hated that his name kept coming up, especially when I was here to clear my mind. My divorce from Mario was brutal. He didn't want to give me one dime. And even though he was the one who had gone out and had a baby with another woman, he did his best to stop me from divorcing him. I still had feelings for him, but I now had a one-mistake rule. Fuck up once, it's over. There were too many men willing and able to do right by me, so for now, I dated whenever I wanted to, screwed whenever I had an urge and enjoyed my single status. In no way did I need a man to make me feel complete. Since I couldn't be with the one I had always wanted to be with, this was now my reality.

Now that the president had arrived, I figured I'd better go put on something to cover up my revealing bikini. I had no idea who would be here, but to see the president was a real shock to me. Jada kept trying to stir up shit by asking who didn't like who. And as they started to discuss what had happened the last time, I stood to leave the room. Jaylin's name had come up again. I simply didn't want to hear it.

"Where are you going?" Keith asked. He had been sitting next to me, and the smell of his masculine cologne made me think of Mario. It was apparent that Keith had money—how much was the big question?

"I'm going to the bedroom to find something to cover up with. I don't feel comfortable dressed like this in front of the president."

Jada clapped her hands. "Thank you!" she shouted. "Thank you, Jesus, for doing all that you do!"

I ignored her and listened to Keith. His eyes were mesmerizing, but they also came with a warning.

"I don't see why you feel as if you need to change. We're all going to swim around here, and I assume the president has swimming trunks as well."

"Probably so," Evelyn said to Keith as she teased the bangs on her forehead with her fingers. "But I think it would be smart for her to, at least, cover up. That bikini is a bit much."

Who was she to tell me my bikini was a bit much? Some women needed to keep their mouths shut. She was lucky that I wasn't in the mood to say what was on my mind out loudly. Instead, I walked away and went into the bedroom. As I entered the closet, I heard someone come into the room. I wasn't sure who it was, until I stepped out of the closet and saw Keith standing by the door.

"I apologize for seeming a little aggressive, but I wanted to let you know how much I think you got it going on. There is something about beautiful women that just takes me there. I don't mind expressing myself when I'm in the presence of a woman like you."

"Thanks for your kind words, Keith, and trust me when I say I appreciate your compliments. I can be a bit aggressive too, so forgive me if I ever come across too strong."

I entered the closet again, removing a sheer black wrap I often wore around my bikini bottoms to cover up. I tied it around my waist while leaving the closet. Keith remained close to the door, but he was sitting on the bed closest to it.

"So, tell me about yourself," he said, wringing his hands together. "Are you married, engaged, taken, available, not interested . . . what?"

I walked his way and sat on the bed across from him, crossing my legs.

"I'm not sure how to answer your question yet, so why don't you tell me what's up with you first?"

His eyes scanned my legs then he shifted them to the floor, as if he was in deep thought. That let me know instantly that he wasn't prepared to answer me either. But within a few more seconds, he lifted his head and spoke up.

"I've been engaged for about a year or so now. I'm unsure about the woman I've been on-and-off with, because she's been real confused about who or what she really wants. I have a difficult time dealing with people who can't make up their minds, also with women who are dishonest. We have a child together, so I'm trying to see if we can get things to work for the sake of our child."

"It wouldn't be wise to hang on for the sake of the kid, but I do understand why so many people do it. I also have a hard time dealing with people who can't make up their minds, especially when they already know, deep down, who or what they really want."

Keith nodded, and as he went on to tell me more about his background, I inspected him all over. The colorful tattoos on his arms told me he was a creative man. His narrow eyes showed hurt. The way he spoke was sexy, but the sadness took over his voice. Even though he was handsome and stable moneywise, I knew that after one night of sex with him I would break his heart even more. I was very particular about who I gave my goodies to these days, and unfortunately, Keith would be a step down for me. With that being said, who knew what would happen in this house? He definitely had my attention for now.

"Are you here for money, business or pleasure," he flat out asked me.

"I'm not exactly sure yet. Ask me that in about another week or two."

We both laughed, and when the door opened, both of our heads snapped to the side. In walked the president. This time he was alone.

"Sorry to interrupt, but I need to remove a few items from my luggage."

"No need to apologize," I said, standing up. So did Keith. "We were just leaving to go outside for a swim. After you get settled in, hopefully, you'll have time to join us."

With his hands dipped into his pockets, he nodded. "Maybe so. We'll see."

I let Keith exit first, and when I turned to see if the president was watching us, he wasn't. He had gone into the closet, carrying one of his bags with him.

When Keith and I returned to the living room area, all eyes were fixed in our direction. I figured everyone must've thought we'd been in the bedroom hooking up, and the person with the tightest face was Evelyn. I wasn't sure what her connection was to Keith, but I'd heard her mention something about her best friend. In no way did I come here to interfere with anyone's relationship, but in my opinion, it was always left up to the man to decide if he was willing to take the risk. That went for married man too, but whatever. I mean, Roc was fine as hell—too fine—but that ring on his finger kept flashing at me every time he'd said something to me. The ring made me think about Mario, about what he'd done and how unfortunate it was that I had to end things. A ring was just a ring, I guess, and I was shocked to see the president wasn't wearing one.

The whole world knew he had issues with his marriage. It had been in the news almost every single day, and the last thing I'd heard was the first lady had moved out of the White House. I'd also heard she moved back in, but there weren't many media outlets reporting that. I assumed he was here because, like all of us, he needed to get away for a while and chill. I wasn't sure if Hell House would allow him the level of peace or privacy he needed, and according to the paperwork I'd received from the producers, there was a chance this could all wind up on TV. It hadn't been confirmed, but it was a possibility. How he would ever be able to explain why he was here, I wasn't sure, even though he was so good at explaining things via TV.

"I'm glad you came out of that room," Chase said in a slick tone as she eyed the bikini I still had on. "I thought the president had locked the door and the three of you were indulging yourselves."

I quickly let her know that was *not* what I was about.

"That's not really my thing, and after speaking to Keith, he doesn't seem like the kind of man who would be a willing participant to anything like that. Maybe you would be, and that's your prerogative. I'm not knocking you one bit. Just making it clear that it's not for me."

Chase ignored my comment and started to put on more red lipstick, as if she needed more. She didn't even need all of that foundation she'd had on, and, hopefully, by tomorrow it would all be gone.

"I can't speak for Keith," Roc said. "But just about every nigga I know would be down for a threesome, particularly when two women are involved."

Keith agreed, but said he wasn't interested in going there "at the moment."

"A big no for me, if we're talking about the president being involved," Keith said. "I already feel a little uncomfortable around him, and I'm not sure how to conduct myself with him being here. Never in my wildest dream did I expect this."

Everyone else agreed, with the exception of Roc and Jada.

"Him being here don't bother me one bit," Roc said, shrugging his shoulders. "Be your fucking self. I'm sure he would want us to be."

"I agree. It is what it is," Jada said while stirring something in a bowl. "I'm baking y'all a cake, and once I put it in the oven, I'm gon' make y'all some of those little summer rolls that look like eggrolls. I'll whip up some ham fried rice too. It should take me about another hour or so to have everything done. We're having fried chicken for dinner. I hope y'all like chicken, and if you don't, please raise your hand."

Nobody raised their hand, but Evelyn questioned what a summer roll was.

"It's an eggroll that you eat in the summertime," Jada said with a twisted face. "I mean, what kind of stupid question is that?"

"I thought it was a spring roll, no matter what season you eat it in," Evelyn replied.

Jada stopped stirring the batter and sighed. "Let me get a few things straight around here, before I have to punch somebody in the face. I say some fucked-up shit sometimes, but please don't correct me, especially when y'all already know what I mean. I'm not the only one who say things that don't add up, and even my friend with a Ph.D. get the words they, their, and they're mixed up sometimes. Get over it and move on."

Jada had a real slick mouth, but I kind of liked her. She kept it real, no matter what. Chase and Evelyn appeared taken aback by her tone, but it didn't bother me as much. The two of them, however, did. I hadn't put my finger completely on it just yet, but their continuous stares and comments already told me that I damn well needed to watch my back.

Roc

St. Louis was small. Everybody knew somebody that I knew like the back of my hand. The president had quite a reputation in the streets. Nobody ever predicted that he would occupy the Oval Office one day, but only stupid motherfuckers counted out black men who were not only street smart, but book smart too. I was proud of the brotha. Real proud, and with him being older than I was, he was definitely somebody I could look up to and learn a few things from. I wanted to hear all about those White House stories we'd been hearing on the news, and right after we chowed down on the rice and spring rolls Jada hooked up, we sat outside chilling. Scorpio and Chase were in the pool, while Evelyn and Jada sat on the edge, hollering at each other. They all seemed to get along just fine. Compared to last time, this was a miracle. I wasn't up to swimming just yet and neither was Keith or the president. We sat in several of the lounging chairs, talking about each of our personal lives that seemed chaotic for the prez and Keith. Me, on the other hand, I was good. Bump all that flirting shit from earlier. My eyes peeped what they were supposed to, and hella fine or not, none of these ladies, not one, had anything on Desa Rae. She was my baby. I loved her ass to death. She could be a mutha at times, but all-in-all, we'd been doing well. Our daughter, Chassidy, meant the world to me, as did Li'l Roc. I was missing them already, but once a year, Dez and me decided to take vacations without each other. We agreed that space was important in a marriage. She wasn't really down with the idea of this Hell House shit, and all she said was for me to decide. I made a decision to be here, knowing that I was taking a risk by coming back to St. Louis, The Lou, period. Some tragic things had happened, causing me to jet and never look back. But last week when I got in, I stopped by a few places to let niggas know I was still alive and to say what's up. Many people thought I was dead; those closest to me knew otherwise. I sometimes got bored living in another country, but as long as Desa Rae was with me, how could I go wrong?

"Very good," Keith said, referring to the fried rice Jada had cooked. "I didn't think it would turn out like that. She did the damn thing for sure."

"Honestly," the prez said with his hands locked behind his head. Keith and I had changed into shorts, but the prez had on slacks and a button-down shirt that was slightly opened. "I was surprised by the rice too. Been a long time since I tasted rice that good, and now that I'm away from Washington D.C., I hope someone can find it in their heart to bring me a whole order of special fried rice from that place on West Florissant Avenue. I forgot the name of it, but they used to have some of the best rice ever."

"Man, you talking about Northland Chop Suey," I said, licking my lips. "They be hooking a nigga up down there. I haven't eaten there in years, but from what I heard, they're still in business."

"Yes, they are," Keith confirmed. "Trina and I were there a few weeks ago. They have the best hot braised chicken, and the truth is, you can't go wrong with anything on the menu, not even the fish."

I glanced at the ladies, again, who still seemed to be having a good time. "Speaking of items on the menu, I have to ask y'all how we gon' be able to stay up and not go down when it comes to these fine women in the house. We struggled real bad last time. This time, I want to know if the two of you foresee some problems."

I really couldn't get a feel for the prez yet, but I already knew who Keith was down with. He had been watching her all day, and while she was in the swimming pool, he couldn't keep his eyes off her.

They both remained quiet while studying the women who were now laughing. "For me," Keith said then took a deep breath. "Normally, I would go for a woman like Chase. She's more of my type and she got that petite and tight body like Trina's. But I sense something weird about Chase already. She got this . . . this look about her that scares me, so I'm going to keep my distance. Evelyn's sweet, she's nice looking too, but she has major issues. Our history would never allow me to go there, and besides, she's Trina's friend. Scorpio, however, maaaan, I don't know what to say, other than she defines sexy. It's the kind of sexy she can display even when she may not be trying. A sexy where she can have a do-rag on her head, dirty clothes on and still look good. I'm feeling her, for sure, but more than anything I'm here to have a good time, not to necessarily pick up women."

The prez seemed reluctant to answer so I spoke up before he did.

"You are one hundred percent correct about Chase, and trust me when I say you don't want to go there. I did, and it was one of the biggest mistakes of my life. I found out she was my wife's half-sister. The fallout from that shit wasn't pretty."

"What?" Keith said, cocking his head back.

"You're kidding me," added the prez. "Didn't you know they were related, before you made a decision to go there?"

"Naw, unfortunately not. But it all worked out. Meanwhile, Chase is a mutha. She burned down one dude's crib and she tried to come after me too. I wasn't having it and neither was my wife. Aside from her, Jada is straight up me. She is fun as hell, and we used to get high as fuck around here. That's no disrespect to you, Mr. Prez; after all, I heard how you used to get down too. But, uh, if it wasn't for her fucked up attitude, her bossy ways and all the foolishness she brings, yeah, I would've gone there, instead of with Chase. Scorpio is the sexiest, but I can tell she got the kind of game that can shut a nigga down. Evelyn doesn't really move me, but that's just my take on things."

"Evelyn seems . . . sweet," the prez said. "Very attractive, but demanding."

"Demanding is putting it mildly," Keith said. "I could tell you some stories about her, long enough to write a book. Stories that you wouldn't believe, but if she stabs her BFF's in the back, you'd better watch yours."

"Well, demanding may not be the appropriate term, but sneaky for sure. I haven't had enough time to read the others yet, and my number one rule is to never speculate too much about people. But I do know that Jada can cook. I may have to take her back to the White House with me."

We laughed and when Jada turned her head to look at us, I rushed up from behind, pushing her in the swimming pool. She made a huge splash, especially when she kept flopping her arms around in the water, as if she couldn't swim.

"He . . . hel . . . helllllp!" she shouted as she went up and down in the water. I thought she was playing; so did everyone else. We all laughed, until she went under water and stayed there. I went into panic mode and jumped in the water to get her. As I carried her limp and heavy body out of the water, Keith helped me lay her down on the concrete pavement.

"Oh my God," Evelyn shouted with tears in her eyes. "Is she going to be alright?"

"Maybe I should call 911," Scorpio said in a panicky voice. "Does anybody have a cell phone?"

Chase and I knew Jada liked to bullshit around a lot, but it didn't appear that she was breathing. The prez removed his shirt, and as he leaned over Jada, pumping her chest a few times, there was no movement. I started to feel as if this was no joke.

"Move, man," I said to the prez, trying to shove him away. "Let me see what I can do."

He ignored me and started to perform CPR on Jada. With his mouth covering hers, she laid there like a dead woman. My heart pounded against my chest, and when I looked around, I could see tears trapped in all of the lady's eyes.

"Who has a cell phone?" Keith asked. "Anybody?"

Nobody had one, but just as Scorpio sprinted toward the sliding doors, Jada started rubbing the back of the prez's head, moaning as she gripped it tight to hold his mouth over hers. He quickly backed away, looking at her as he wiped his lips.

"Daaaaamn," Jada said, lifting her head. "Yo lips soft and juicy. I feel a whole lot better now. Thank you for saving my life!"

I could have kicked Jada's ass. Nobody laughed, and with frustrated looks on our faces, we all went inside, leaving her outside to think about how foolish something like that was. As we all sat on the sofa, many shaking our heads, she came inside, trying to explain her actions.

"I was only playing, damn. If y'all boring ass people want to have attitudes, so doggone what. Too bad, and when all is said and done, I still can say that I had the pleasure of kissing the president. None of y'all can say that, so bye. Cook for y'all selves and don't ask me to do nothing else around here."

She marched off to the bedroom, acting like the brat she was. Hell, no, I would never fuck with a chick like her, and after seeing her in action again, to me, she had gotten worse.

Chase

That stupid bitch, Jada, was at it again. I didn't even know why she was here, and what kind of host was she? I don't know who invited her to come here, but if I had anything to say about it, she would be out of here soon. We just didn't need the extra drama this time, and even though I didn't like the majority of people here, I was trying my best to get along with everyone.

That, in itself, was hard. I wasn't a forgiving person, so when it came to Jada and Roc, I cringed every time I looked at them. I hoped that Jada had really drowned, but I knew she was faking. She wanted to be the center of attention and she liked to get everybody all flustered about her. That was the kind of person she was and had always been. When it came to her cooking, it was just alright to me. Everybody boasted about it, I assumed, just to make her feel good. I wasn't sure how long I would be able to tolerate her, nor was I sure how long I would be able to play the pretend game with Roc. I couldn't believe how nice he was trying to be. There was no way in hell he fucked me the way he did, and, now, it wasn't a big deal because he was married to my sister. I hadn't forgotten about any of it, and I intended to play this game and play it well. Thus far, I did like Keith, and the president was definitely on my good side. I could actually see myself screwing him, but I wasn't sure how I was going to approach the situation. Keith would be easy. He had 'I got problems' written all over him. I would probably just fuck him to warm up things a bit, but my ultimate goal would be the president. What a catch that would be, huh?

As for Scorpio and Evelyn, please. First off, that bitch Scorpio annoyed me. She'd been walking around like she was the queen of England, then again, what an insult that was to the queen who had morals and values. In my opinion, a real woman didn't have to show all her goodies to get attention. So what her ass was big. So what her face was pretty. So what she had kids with Jaylin, lived in a mansion, and so what she had the men's attention. When you put yourself out there like she had, why wouldn't they chase after her? She was already a piece of work. I couldn't wait to shut her down when I tell her how well her baby's daddy screwed me on the hood of his car. I'll never forget how good Jaylin was to me that day, and I would put any amount of money on it that she didn't know a damn thing about it. I also predicted that my news would disturb her—it was my goal to upset her and get her out of here as quickly as I could. I sensed that she wanted to make a move on the president; then again, I could be wrong. I had to pay more attention to her, as I did to Evelyn who seemed to be a cute, airhead ho with no brains. Kind of like the first lady was. That was why her husband was here, very vulnerable and probably open to whatever. My kind of man for sure.

"Just because Jada isn't going to cook," I said, getting off the sofa. "It doesn't mean we won't eat. I can cook, and I'm sure some of you can too, right?"

"Count me out," Scorpio said, proudly. "I have a housemaid who takes care of all of that for me and my children. And trust me when I say I didn't come here to cook."

See. All she was good for was lying on her back and screwing. What kind of woman admitted, in front of a bunch of men, that she didn't cook? She didn't even notice the look on the president's face when she'd said it. I could tell that was a big, fat negative for him.

"I'll help," Roc said. "Desa Rae be hooking me up and she done taught me how to whip up a whole lot of dishes in the kitchen."

Evelyn offered to help too, but when she stood up, she questioned not only who Desa Rae was, but who Jaylin was as well.

"I keep hearing their names, but who are those people?"

Roc didn't bother to answer so I had to speak up for him. "Desa Rae is Roc's wife, and Jaylin was here last time. He's now married to his high school sweetheart, right Scorpio?"

Ouch. I knew it stung, but I couldn't help it.

"That would be incorrect," she said. "He knew her way before high school and—

"And just because he's married that don't mean shit," Jada said, exiting the bedroom and walking toward the kitchen. "You trying to be messy, Chase, but we all know that Jaylin and marriage don't go well together. Stop trying to upset that woman. Truth be told, I don't really think she cares." Jada looked at Scorpio for confirmation. "Do you?"

Scorpio rolled her eyes and cleared her throat. "Allow me to set the record straight around here, please. I don't want to discuss Jaylin, and quite frankly, I'm tired of hearing his name. I didn't come here to discuss my ex-husband, Mario, either, so please do not ask me anymore questions about either one of them."

I couldn't resist a response. "Sounds like you're still bitter about them both. From my experience with men, and from what I do know *personally* about Jaylin, I recommend that you try your best to move on and not be so hurt about losing him to the same woman."

Jada shook her head. "Girl, you are still real messy, ain't you? I thought we could all relax and have a little fun around here this time around, but you really trying to start something with *Jaylin's ex.*"

"I'm not trying to start anything. I'm just speaking the truth, as I always do."

Scorpio stood, looking at me with a smirk on her face. "Jada, you don't need to say anything at all to Chase about being messy. She knows what she is, as do you. Chase also knows what it feels like to be the real bitter bitch in the house, and that, unfortunately, you really and truly are."

"Do we really have to insult each other like this?" Evelyn said. "As women, we have to do better. We need to start lifting each other up, instead of tearing each other down. If Scorpio doesn't want to hear anything about her exes, then please stop talking about them. I wouldn't want to hear about my exes either, and, Chase, I'm sure you wouldn't want to hear about yours."

"None of us want to discuss them," the president said, standing and stretching his arms. Apparently, he'd heard enough bickering from us. "So from this moment on, let's try our best to respect each other's wishes and have ourselves a magnificent time. In reference to cooking dinner, I would love to help out too. Just let me know what I can do to get things started."

I loved how the president intervened to calm the situation. Roc or Keith didn't say anything. Obviously, they were waiting on a cat fight—they almost got one. Instead, I invited the president to come help. But right as he started moving this way, Jada opened her big mouth.

"This is my kitchen, and I will not have people in here doing what they don't know how to do. Please exit and go sit down. No disrespect, Mr. President, but stick to issues in the White House, cause I got this. I was upset a few minutes ago, but when I'd thought about it, I apologize for acting the way I did. Plus, a sista like me still gotta eat."

Jada shooed us out of the kitchen, and when we returned to the sofa, I made sure that I sat as close as I could to the president. He was listening to Jada rant about how *errrrbody* needed to stay out of her kitchen. I truly wondered what in the heck he thought of her.

"You've convinced me not to ever enter the kitchen again," he said to her with a smile. "As long as we all get something to eat for dinner, I'm okay with sitting right here."

"I hope so," Jada replied. "Because I'm gon' fix you something real special tonight for saving my life. Y'all probably thought I was strictly playing, but there was a little something clogged in my throat. After you blew in it, it cleared the passageway."

All he did was nod. Was probably thinking how stupid she was to himself, and I'm sure he wasn't happy about her desperate attempt to kiss him. I also wanted to taste his tongue, and in due time I would.

"Anybody want to go shoot some pool with me while Jada cook dinner?" Roc asked, looking around.

Evelyn stood, straightening her bikini top that barely covered her firm but fake titties. Unlike Scorpio, Evelyn had on a short robe that covered her butt.

"I do, Roc," she said. "Let's go to the game room."

After they walked off, Scorpio stood her near-naked ass up, making an announcement so she could be seen.

"I'm going to take a shower and change clothes. It has been a long day, and after I get something to eat, it'll be time for me to get some beauty rest."

Did we really need to know about her damn beauty rest?

Keith snapped his finger. "I was getting ready to go take a shower too. You beat me to it."

"We can flip a coin," Scorpio said. "If you win, I'll let you go first."

"Naw, that's okay. Ladies first. You go ahead and do your thing. I'll get one later."

"Thanks. But if you want to come wash my back, you can."

Keith appeared shock by what she'd said; then again, so was I. Even the president was, but Scorpio was serious as ever. I couldn't believe when Keith followed her into the bathroom, closing the door behind them.

"Oooookay," I said with a slight laugh. "I didn't think it would be that easy, but some women have no respect for themselves. With that being said, Mr. President, how are you?"

"I'm fine, but please do away with calling me Mr. President while I'm here. Call me Stephen."

I touched my chest, flattered that he'd made the suggestion.

"I have too much respect for you to call you anything other than the president. So I hope you don't mind me saying it, because it seems like the appropriate thing to do."

"You can call me whatever you want to. I—"

"As long as it ain't her baby's daddy," Jada shouted from the kitchen. "I'm just saying."

I sighed and cut my eyes at her. The tone of my voice lowered as I continued my conversation with the president.

"What were you saying?" I asked.

"Stephen is my name, so feel free to use it. But I won't be upset with you for calling me Mr. President. I've kind of gotten used to it."

"I know it must have taken a while for you to get used to, and how does it feel living in the White House? I could sit here all night and talk to you about what's really been going on, but I know you came here so you didn't have to address all of that."

"I don't mind talking about some things, but many things I'd rather not get into. What is something specific you'd like to know?"

I'd heard so much on the news about him that I didn't even know where to start. "Well, for starters, how do you like being the president? What are some of your biggest challenges, and are you and the first lady getting a divorce? Also, what about your mother? The media is forever talking about her, and who really killed the vice president? Lastly, how are you able to come here when there is so much unfinished business at the White House? I know you don't trust the new vice president, and to me, she comes off as real racist. Is she?"

The president crossed his legs and chuckled. He was so damn sexy, and being this close to him made me feel real special. I loved how calm, cool and collected he was. He made all of us feel as if we were on his level, and not once had he said anything disrespectful to anyone.

"You crammed a lot of questions in there, but I'll be happy to answer a few of them for you. I enjoy being the president, but my biggest challenges have been with the people closest to me. I've had numerous problems with people who are supposed to be my biggest supporters, but their level of disrespect has shocked me in a major way. Job related, my biggest problems are dealing with terrorism, the economy and racism. Our country is on a backward path, and to me, that's a big disappointment. The first lady and I aren't getting a divorce and my mother is the sweetest woman in the world. You can't believe everything you hear from the media—they tend to fabricate many false stories."

"I figured that, but whatever your reason is for being here, I'm glad you came. I hope we have an opportunity to get to know each other a little better, and if there is anything . . . anything I can do to make your stay here more pleasurable, be sure to let me know."

The smile on his face was enough to let me know that I was in there.

Keith

I was in a daze. Couldn't believe Scorpio had asked me to wash her back, and there I was, with a hard-on like never before, standing there doing exactly what she asked me to do. As she faced the wall, her back was to me. Soap suds and water ran down her curvaceous body and into her crack that was surrounded by two perfect sized mountains. She allowed me to touch them. Gave me permission to tackle her whole body with a soapy rag, and as I stood outside of the small shower honoring her request, I had to ask what was it about me that she appeared to gravitate toward.

"I know a decent man when I see him," she said, holding her hair aside so I could wash the nape of her neck. "I didn't mean to catch you off guard like this, but I had to be fair, especially since you wanted to take a shower too."

"You didn't have to be so generous." I squeezed the rag, watching the soap and water rain down her body again. "And if I ask you to wash me when you're done, will you do it?"

She laughed and turned to face me. Breasts were firm and perfect. Nipples I could suck on all day, and her shaved pussy had the fabric of my jeans stretched as far as it could go, as my dick threatened to break loose. My eyes shifted back to her face; I awaited an answer. Hopefully, it would be the right answer, so I could hurry out of my clothes and step into the shower with her.

"I would love to return the favor and wash you as well, but I have to ask you something, Keith. If you get naked and get into the shower with me, what do you anticipate will happen?"

I didn't hesitate to answer. "Exactly what I hope will happen. You and I will have sex."

"And then what? I'm asking because I've been here too many times before. Had my heart broken and have broken the hearts of others, especially when they seem so eager to indulge in sex, simply because it seems to be a cure for the moment. With you, I sense that sex between us would only be a quick cure for you. That sex with me would be for revenge or because you feel it would make you and the woman you're engaged to equal. You don't have to answer me, if you don't want to, but I want you to think real hard about this, before you remove your clothes and get in here with me."

Scorpio and I had been conversing more than anyone, so I figured she had read between the lines, pertaining to my relationship with Trina. Yes, she had disappointed me, time and time again. Her last trip to New York to go see another woman she was interested in had totally upset me. I hadn't been able to put it behind me ever since. Even when she got pregnant with our child, I still couldn't come to grips with what she'd done. There were too many lies being told, and to this day, I wasn't even sure if she wanted to be with a woman or if she still wanted to be with me. She claimed all she needed was me. Begged me to get back with her, after her failed attempt to get with the woman in New York. I just didn't trust her, but I loved her so much that I proposed to her. I kept telling myself that we would, eventually, work things out. That things would get better. But deep in my heart, I just didn't know. I didn't know what it would take for me to forgive her lies and somehow make our relationship work.

"I have to give you credit for reading me so well," I said to Scorpio who knew that sex with her would be about revenge. "My heart has been broken, and for the past year or so, I've had many of debates with myself about who or what I really want. Sex between us would be . . . sex. Good sex, for sure, and I'm glad you asked me the question 'then what' because that's part of my answer."

Scorpio reached for the faucet to turn off the water. "I figured that much, and even though I know this isn't the beginning of a special relationship, I just wanted you to give some thought to why you were willing to go there so soon with me."

"Because you're sexy as hell, that's why. And, to be honest, it has been a looong time since I've gotten this kind of reaction from my friend down below. That may sound unbelievable, but it's the truth."

I backed up as Scorpio stepped out of the shower. There was a thick towel hanging on a rack, so I reached for it, giving it to her.

"Thanks," she said, drying herself with the towel. "But a woman being sexy should never be the sole reason why a man wants to have sex with her so quickly. There are numerous sexy women in this world. Are you going to pursue every last one of them that you see, or are you going to find a way to deal with your broken heart, first, and then decide who or what you really want? You're accusing Trina of being confused. But when you take a step back and look at it, Keith, maybe you are too."

"I'm not confused at all. Well, in the moment I am and I get everything you're saying. As for the sexy woman thing, I haven't pursued anyone, other than you. I've been faithful to Trina, but I don't know how much longer that's going to last."

"Don't get upset with me for saying this, but I don't believe, for one minute, that I'm the first sexy woman you've pursued during your troubled relationship. You came on too strong. I knew instantly that something was very wrong."

I hated that she could read me like this, but whatever. There was another woman, my ex, but she also told me to do some soul searching before I'd made a move her way again.

"I won't say if you're wrong or right, but I will say thanks for the conversation. I needed it, and I'd better wash my own self—for now anyway."

Scorpio smiled. "Yes. For now, please do. As we travel down this long journey together, in this crazy little house, let me know if I can help in any other way."

"Will do," I said as she walked to the door. Before she left, though, I moved forward and reached for her arm. She turned and I grabbed her waist, pulling her to me. "If we're not going to have sex, at least allow me to do this."

I leaned in to taste her lips. Her tongue slipped into my mouth, and as we indulged ourselves for about a minute, I had the pleasure of holding her ass in my hands, massaging it. My dick was overly excited, but when Scorpio backed away from me, I felt it deflate just a little. She placed her hand on my chest, feeling the fast pace of my heartbeat.

"Go ahead and take your shower. I'll see you when you're done."

After she left, I stripped naked and took the longest cold shower I'd ever had.

Nearly an hour later, I had finished my shower, changed clothes and joined the others in the living room area. The president and Chase were playing cards, Jada was setting the table for dinner and I saw Scorpio sitting outside by the pool. I wasn't sure if Roc and Evelyn were still in the game room, but just as I got ready to go outside to see what was up, Jada called my name.

"What's up?" I asked while standing by the sliding doors.

"Did you and Scorpio do the nasty in the bathroom?"

I was taken aback by her question. She didn't know me well enough to ask me that question, and quite frankly, I wasn't too keen about the way she conducted herself around here. It was one thing to be funny, but Jada was rude, obnoxious and too damn ghetto for me.

"I don't know what the nasty is. If you're asking if we had sex, that's really none of your business."

"To be honest, yes it is. I need to know everything that goes on in this house, and if you've already managed to get that little penis of yours wet, I wanna know. So did you or didn't you?"

This chick was crazy. My face twisted as I looked at her, trying to respond to her as I would any woman.

"First of all, my penis isn't little. Second, you don't need to know shit about me. Lastly, watch how you speak to me going forward, because I'm not the one to sit around playing childish games with ignorant, no class women."

"Nigga, don't make me hurt your feelings. Just because you done got you some pussy from the prettiest bitch in the house, it doesn't mean you can speak to me any way you wish. I suggest you go outside, regroup and rethink how you gon' holla at me going forward. I only asked you one little question. You act like I asked you for some food stamps or something."

I didn't have time for this chick, so I didn't bother to respond. Instead, I went outside and headed to the game room where I saw Roc and Evelyn tossing back drinks while playing pool. I decided to join them, until dinner got done. Hopefully, Jada wouldn't poison my food.

Evelyn

Being with Roc was too fun. He was real laid back, full of energy and one fine specimen period. I observed him the whole time we were in the game room. Actually, I'd had my eyes on him ever since I'd entered this house. I appreciated men who were a little rough around the edges, and he was that and then some. Too bad he was married though. He kept mentioning his wife, but I wasn't sure if he was doing it to get a reaction from me or not. There was a time when having sex with a married man was no biggie for me. Hell, I'd screwed my best friend's husband, Cedric, but I wound up killing his ass for getting too out of line. I did time in jail for my actions, and ever since I'd been out, things had been a little different for me. I gave more thought to my actions, and when it came to men, I tried my best to keep my distance from the married ones.

Roc, however, shook up something inside of me. So did the president, but he was at a level that I didn't dare want to touch. I'd been there and done that with Keith's father. After what that man had done to me, I told myself I would never deal with another man who had authority the way he did. He did something with the CIA—something that allowed him to have too much power and control over me. I suspected the president had that kind of control as well, so I intended to stay in my lane this time and let Scorpio and Chase have at it.

Pertaining to those two, I can honestly say that I didn't have many feelings about them yet. I could sense they weren't going to get along, and like most women who didn't, it seemed to have something to do with a man. Scorpio seemed a bit more sensible than Chase, but she also seemed like one of those uppity chicks who thought they were so much better than other people. It was evident that she was wealthy. There was a rich, polished look about her, and when she mentioned her housemaid, that pretty much confirmed how she was living. Chase was the jealous type, but as attractive as she was, she really didn't have to be. She seemed to be in competition more than any of us, and I guess we were, considering that we were all here to win some money. Jada was supposed to provide us with more details about the money. Thus far, she hadn't. There were a few things about her that bothered me, but for now, I intended to keep my mouth shut and go with the flow.

While Roc and I had taken a break from shooting pool and were sitting at the bar drinking, Keith had entered the room. He and Roc were now indulged in a competitive game while I watched. There was a time when I wanted a piece of Keith. I thought he wanted me too, but when I attempted to act on what I thought could've been possible, he made it clear that he was down with my best friend, Trina. That was then, though. Now, they had a lot of problems. I always felt as if Keith could do better than Trina, only because she had taken advantage of his love for her. She toyed with his emotions and had broken his heart. So many women would love to have a man like him, and from what I had always known about Keith, he was the real deal. He treated Trina good . . . real good. I guessed being faithful to her, paying the bills, keeping a roof over her head, giving her money to shop, supporting her career . . . none of that was good enough for her. Now, he was in a very vulnerable state. A state that had me thinking and feeling as if I needed to pursue him again. Yes, Trina was my BFF, but she was wrong. Wrong for doing him the way she had, and whenever we talked about it, it seemed as if she hadn't regretted all that she'd done. I hated that about her. Her lack of regret made me eager to shake things up with Keith. Neither of my BFF's trusted me around their men, and they had every reason not to, considering all that had happened. But if Keith and I got together, I honestly did not think Trina would care. It was as if she wanted him to leave her. I wondered how she would feel if he left her for me?

My eyes shifted from Roc to Keith as they continued to shoot pool. I couldn't go wrong with either of them. Roc seemed like he was capable of setting some shit off in the bedroom. He had that thug thing going on, and I could see his lips working wonders between my legs. He and Keith had numerous tattoos on their bodies—Keith's were more decorative. His stallion-like frame towered over Roc's only by a few inches, and I loved men who weren't so serious all the time, particularly like Keith's father was. That was another little problem for me. Keith had been upset with me for getting involved with his father. He also didn't like me for interfering in his relationship with Trina, but over time, he came around. As my friendship with Trina mended, he opened up to me again. I was thankful to him for that, so I had to be real careful not to get on his bad side.

I tossed back the remaining alcohol in my glass, and then I left the game room to go see what else was going on. As soon as I reached the door, Roc called after me.

"Where you going?" he asked. "I thought you was gon' let me spank that ass again."

"You can spank my ass any time you want to. Whenever you're ready, so am I."

I winked and he laughed. I did, too, but my words were based on facts. Right when I left the game room, I saw Scorpio lying back on one of the lounging chairs with her arm resting across her forehead and a book in her hand. She seemed to be all into it, so I didn't want to interrupt her. Instead, I went inside to see what was up with dinner. Jada was setting the table; I offered to help.

"Nope," she said, moving her head from side-to-side. "I don't need nobody's help with this. I'll be done in about five minutes, so go let the others know if they want to eat, they'd better get in here."

I looked at the delicious smelling food on the table and had to give credit when it was due. The crispy fried chicken looked mouthwatering, as did the whipped potatoes with butter. A chocolate cake was in the center of the table, and a salad with all the good toppings was next to it. There were even dinner rolls on the table. I wasn't sure if Jada had homemade them or not.

"Everything looks and smells delicious. I'm not a bad cook, but it's been a while since I cooked like this. You must have a whole lot of kids or a grandmother who taught you well."

Just that fast, Jada snapped at me. "Do I look like I got any kids to you? Just because I'm healthy, it don't mean I got a gang of kids somewhere. I don't have any children at all, and all my grandmother taught me was how not to be a crackhead. I taught myself everything I know, okay?"

If I replied to her, an argument would ensue. I ignored her, and when I looked at Chase and the president, who appeared to be enjoying each other's company, they had ignored her too. I walked outside, telling Scorpio dinner was ready and I also informed Keith and Roc. They all said they were coming, but Jada got upset when Keith and Roc had taken too long to come inside.

"I hate ungrateful muthafuckas," she said, pouting as the rest of us waited at the table. "This food gon' get cold if we keep waiting, and after all of my hard work, the least they could do is be on time."

"Maybe they're in the middle of a competitive game and can't pull themselves away," the president said. "I say let's eat. I would love the opportunity to delve into dinner and conversation with four beautiful black women, all by myself."

We all smiled, and after a quick prayer, we started to eat and converse with each other. The president was more down to earth than I'd thought he was, and when we started talking about the state of our country, he was all in.

"It's terrifying and many people have lost hope. My administration hasn't done enough to stop the bleeding, but we are making progress. A whole lot of damage has been done over the years, and the recovery will take a long time. Longer than I expected, so I want all of you to be real patient with me, alright?"

"Of course we will, *Stephen*," Chase said, gazing at him as if she was in love. "We all know how difficult things must be for you and we all have your back."

"Stephen," Jada said, cocking her head back. "Girl, don't disrespect that man like that. You need to call him Mr. President and nothing else."

"Just so you know," Chase fired back. "He told me to call him Stephen, so there is no disrespect going on over here."

"Stephen is fine," the president said. "Or whatever suits each of you."

"Well, I think it's disrespectful to call you by your first name," Jada said. "We don't know you like that, and Chase acting like y'all been friends for years. I'ma keep calling you Mr. President, but if you make me mad, I may have to call you something else. I'm just warning you now, just in case."

Jada was a mess. She was also embarrassing—I felt lucky not to have a friend like her. At least the president had a good sense of humor. All he did was laugh. That was until Scorpio asked him a question that was a bit more personal.

"I never thought we would ever see another black president in the Oval Office again, but what is going on with you and the first lady? Don't you think that all of the drama with her overshadows all the good you're trying to do?"

He chewed his food while looking at Scorpio from across the table. His gaze was interesting. I couldn't tell if he was about to go off on her or not.

"Did I say something wrong?" she asked as he continued to stare at her.

He cleared his throat and finally blinked his eyes.

"I don't like to discuss the first lady with anyone, and to be clear . . . everything you see and or hear on television isn't always factual. In a short period of time, I've done more good for this country than my predecessor did in four years. If that's overlooked or overshadowed by what some people deem as drama, those people can kiss my ass."

Scorpio swallowed and sat up straight. We all waited for her to respond and she did. "The first lady is a lucky woman, and I appreciate a man who is protective of his wife. I also appreciate all of the good that you've done for this country, and I am, and will always be, one of your biggest fans, supporters or whatever you prefer to call me."

She stuck the salad fork in her mouth, chewing while looking at him. I thought Chase was the one trying to make a move on the president, but it was apparent that Scorpio was too.

Then again, she could have said that to irritate Chase. The way she rolled her eyes was an indication that she didn't like what Scorpio had said, nor did she like that the president was still looking at Scorpio. Chase quickly opened her mouth to divert his attention back to her.

"We're all fans, and the women at my job love everything about you. They all voted for you, including many of the white people who are some of your biggest supporters. They did, however, take issue with the whole thing regarding that, uh, reporter. You admitted to having sex with her on live TV. We were all like . . . what? Really?"

Jada slammed her hand on the table, causing it to shake. "Girl, I know!" she shouted. "I was watching TV and they were like breaking news, breaking news! The president came on and he, I mean you were like . . . yeaaaah, I fucked that bitch but so damn what! My mouth was wide open, and the two-liter soda I was drinking spilled all over me. I cracked the hell up when I saw the camera pan all of those white people's faces in the room. They didn't know what to say."

The looks on our faces were probably the same. I couldn't believe Jada had spoken so bluntly—neither could the others.

The president shrugged. "I didn't exactly say it like that, but I refused to lie about something that was purposely put out there to embarrass me, or possibly, destroy me. I was surprised by the reaction of the American people. It didn't seem to cause as much damage as my haters thought."

His response enabled me to release the deep breath I'd been holding since Jada's comment. I believed in keeping it real and being yourself, but how could she think that using that kind of foul language around the president was appropriate?

"People didn't care because it ain't like you invented cheating," Jada said. "And from what I know, past presidents have had sex with multiple women. That, uh, Monica Lawooda chick waxed President Clinton real good underneath that desk, and I heard the last president was swinging with his wife. You don't swing with yours, do you? Cause if you do, y'all need to swing in the hood where folks would line up to get a piece of you."

Even though the chicken was good, I'd heard enough. Jada was starting to work me, so I stood and tossed my napkin on the table.

"I'm not that hungry anymore. Save me some cake for later and enjoy the rest of dinner."

I saw Jada pursing her lips and Scorpio chuckled. Chase had a smirk on her face, and I was too embarrassed for Jada to even look at the president's expression. I walked away, heading to the bathroom to wash my hands. After I washed them, I looked in the mirror, teasing my bangs that needed to be bumped up with a curling iron. My skin was blemish free, but my lips were a little dry. I moistened them with my tongue, and when I turned to exit the bathroom, I saw Keith standing in the doorway.

"Are you done?" he asked. "I need to wash my hands before I eat something."

"Yes, I'm done. Who won the game?"

"Unfortunately, Roc did. But after we eat and chill for a bit, I'm sure we'll get another game started. Are you down or not?"

"I'm a little tired, but we'll see. I'll let you know later."

I stepped away from the sink to let Keith wash his hands. While at the door, I called his name and he looked up.

"When you get a moment, I want to talk to you about something important. Just let me know when you have time."

He nodded while looking at me with curiosity in his eyes. I was sure he would inquire soon. At that time, I'd tell him about my desires to hook up with him.

Mr. President

Hell House was exactly what I had expected. There were no surprises here, maybe because I had done my research on every single person in this house, prior to coming here. I had to. I didn't want to put myself in a situation where I was left guessing why this person did this or that, or why they reacted to others in the way they did. My research went back years and years. From Roc's jail time, as well as to Evelyn's, I knew all about it. I knew about Jada's abandonment as a child, the death of her drug dealing boyfriend, to the bi-sexual woman Keith would possibly call his wife. His father was CIA, and unbeknownst to Keith, I knew his father well. Scorpio's profession as a stripper was well known to me, in addition to her recent divorce that provided her with a lifestyle that many people dreamed of. There was no judgement from me whatsoever. It was called life, and whatever path had been chosen for the people here, who was I to look down on them because of my status.

I had made some severe changes in my life, just so I could put myself in the position I was in. But the changes I'd made weren't enough. I'd messed up and brought the wrong people into the White House with me. Trusted people who I had no business trusting. Had my eyes closed when they should have been wide open. The result of those mistakes led me to plotting the death of my V.P., killing one of my best friends, distancing myself from my only son and cheating on my wife who I wholeheartedly felt didn't have my back. The last unfortunate incident at the White House caused me to pack up and leave for a few weeks. Maybe even longer than that, so that was why I was here. I couldn't go to Camp David or any of the other vacation spots presidents normally went to. The media had been on me like flies on shit, and not to many people, with the exception of secret service, knew I was here. Here, having dinner with beautiful black women who had truly been through some shit. Many had made some bad choices . . . severely bad choices, but I was optimistic that everyone would make the necessary changes to better their situations. Even Jada who probably annoyed the hell out of others, but not me. I had a mother who could give her a run for her money, and for the people who had met my mother in person, they knew she was a force to be reckoned with. She didn't know I was here either. I was so sure she was at the White House giving everyone hell about my whereabouts.

After Evelyn left the table, Roc and Keith joined us. We had a good time, and I was delighted to be in the company of more down to earth people. Things got a bit stuffy at the White House at times. There were too many fake and racist people around. I could sense them a mile away. Chase fit the classification of being fake, and she had been going hard all day, trying to say the right things that came off so wrong. I wouldn't dare tell her to correct her approach, and all I did was observe. Everybody and everything. Some people I liked more than others, but I wasn't prepared to say who they were and why. It really didn't matter at this point, especially since Jada had left the table and came back with what she referred to as my 'saving her life' gift. It was a slice of carrot cake, one of my favorites.

"I told you I had your back," she said, smiling as she placed the cake in front me. "I remember somebody mentioning on TV that your favorite kind of cake was carrot cake. It's not homemade, but when I saw the Duncan Hines mix in the cabinet, I couldn't resist."

"I thank you for this, but I told you already about believing what the media tells you. Carrot cake is my least favorite cake. My favorite is pineapple upside down cake."

Jada sighed. Before she could say anything, I told her I was only kidding and that carrot cake was my favorite. "Sometimes," I said, referring to the media. "They do get it right, but it is rare."

She was relieved. She released a deep breath and held her chest.

"I'm glad about that because I was getting ready to say something I would have regretted. Eat your cake, please. I hope you enjoy it."

I picked up the fork to taste it. Tasted pretty good to me, so I thanked Jada again.

"Uh, Jada," Roc said. "Where in the hell is my cake at? My birthday was a couple of weeks ago. I didn't get no cake."

Jada winked and licked across her lips. "Baby, I got more than a piece of cake for your fine ass. You and me been waiting a loooong time to make our dreams a reality and I am competent, I mean confident, that we will do the boogie-woogie soon. Until then, don't be jealous of the president, Boo. He all good, even though he didn't need your vote to put him in office."

"I did vote and I'm sure it helped," Roc said.

Jada threw her hand back at him. "Roc, please. You a convicted felon. Convicted felons can't vote, so stop playing."

Several people laughed, including Roc.

"I am not a convicted felon. And even if I am, I still voted."

"Nigga, quit lying. You didn't get no pardon from the president, and if you did vote, I want to see your voter registration ID right now."

I hurried to silence Jada. "He voted. I assure you he did."

All heads turned in my direction. Jada touched her chest and stuttered. "I . . . I voted too, right?"

"Yes, you voted Democratic. I appreciate your vote."

"I voted Democratic too," Keith said. "Not ashamed to say it, and I voted for you because of your African American status."

"I thank you for your vote, regardless."

My eyes shifted to Chase who studied me, trying to see if I knew how she'd voted. I let her off the hook. "Thanks for your vote, too, and sometimes you have to switch parties."

She smiled. "I did this time, only because I had a lot of faith that you would do the right thing."

The only person sitting at the table I hadn't looked at was Scorpio. She looked at me and shrugged.

"What can I say? I've been a lifetime Republican and I never had much faith in the Democratic Party. Sorry you're on that team, but maybe you'll consider switching parties, since the new and improved V.P. is a Republican woman."

"Girl, shut yo mouth," Jada shouted and slapped the table. "Ain't shit about you conservative and how do you have faith in a

95

party that don't even respect black folks? Y'all fools get on my nerves with that mess. If I was the president, I would reach across the table and slap the shit out of you right now."

"Jada, shut up," Scorpio said. "I vote for whoever I want to, and at the time, I didn't know enough about the president to cast my vote for him. I do, however, regret that I didn't vote for him. He has proven himself to be the best man for the job, and at re-election time, I will cast my next vote for him."

"Don't make me throw up, please," Jada said, sticking out her tongue. "I can't with you, and from this moment on, I need to distance myself from you."

"I feel you on that," Chase added and defensively crossed her arms. "But I guess we forgot that she only *half* black anyway."

For the first time, I witnessed Scorpio lose it. "Both of you bitches can go to hell. I am African American, and my vote is my vote. If don't nobody like it, allow me to turn around so the two of you can kiss my ass. All of it."

Her eyes shifted to me, but I made sure she knew I had no problem with her not voting for me. Things like that used to bother me, but not anymore. I guess if I'd lost, that may be a different story.

"I truly believe in letting people vote and vote for who they wish. Next time, however, for the sake of saving our country, I do hope you get it right."

I was done with dinner, and as the others stayed to converse with each other, I headed outside to take in some fresh air. I kept thinking about what was happening at the White House, and before I knew it, it had gotten pretty late. I couldn't sleep so I went to the theater room to watch movies. The first one was a comedy movie; the other was a war movie. I was very much so indulged while chilling back in the plush, leather chair with my feet propped on an ottoman. My hands were behind my head; I was more relaxed than I had been in months. The movie was almost an hour in, before I looked up and saw someone enter the room. I squinted, trying to see who it was because the room was pretty dark. But when the big screen lit up, I saw Scorpio standing by the door, wrapped in a blanket.

"Everybody was wondering where you had gone to," she said. "They're inside playing Twister and listening to music. Care to join us?"

"No, not tonight. Been a long day and it's now time for me to relax."

She headed toward me. "Is the movie any good?"

"It's okay. It may be quite boring to you though."

Scorpio sat in the leather chair next to me. She removed the blanket, laying it across her lap. Her nightgown was on. It cut right above her knees and was silk. The top part revealed a healthy portion of her firm breasts and her hard nipples poked through the silk fabric.

"I'll watch for a while and then I'll let you know if I think it's boring," she said. "You don't mind, do you?"

"Not at all."

For the next twenty minutes or so, we sat silently watching the movie. She yawned a few times, and I could see her eyelids fading every now and then. It was a long movie, and just as it was almost finished, Scorpio leaned her head on my shoulder and went to sleep. Some of her hair covered her face, and as she released light snores, I kept taking peeks at her. Beautiful she was, but beauty was never enough to move me.

Jada

I couldn't believe that a whole week had gone by and there hadn't been any fights yet. Now, I could have kicked a few people's asses, but since everyone seemed to be getting along, I kept my little issues to myself. I continued to cook delicious foods for everyone, and just last night we had porterhouse steaks, baked potatoes, broccoli with cheese and a whole bunch of wine to top it off. Almost everybody had been getting toasted, with the exception of the president. He said he didn't drink, and he told us an interesting story about his mother being an alcoholic. I really and truly adored the president. Maybe his presence caused everybody to get along, and it sure didn't stop Roc and me from getting high. We had been creeping around getting lit like a mutha. He was my nigga—I swear he was. Lord knows if he wasn't married to Desa Rae, he would be my soulmate. I told him that last night, but as usual, all he did was brush it off. We tried to be discreet with the marijuana, but with the smell all in our clothes, everybody knew what we'd been up to. Even the president, but he didn't say much. All I could say was, this was nothing like the last time. It was a whole lot better, and on a daily basis, I reported to the Alex who I thought should win the million dollars. In return, he reported to me that my money had increased by twenty more thousand dollars. I was good with that.

My decision about the million dollars was based on how I felt that day. One day I was on Roc's team, another day I was for Evelyn. She'd said some nice things about me, and she even apologized for leaving the table that day. Her apology seemed sincere to me, so that was why I voted for her that day. I'd even voted for Keith, even though I sensed that he thought I was too ghetto for him. The only person I did not vote for was Chase. I hated that heifer with a passion. No matter how much I tried, I just couldn't get with her.

She had been all on the president's nuts, but he hadn't paid her much attention. And when she didn't get attention from him, she turned to Keith. The two of them had gotten chummy over the past few days, but I also noticed that him and Evelyn had gotten close as well. I questioned that because her best friend was supposed to be engaged to him. In my opinion, something wasn't right. Evelyn kept watching his every move, and when Scorpio admitted that she and Keith hadn't gotten their freak on in the bathroom that day, both Chase and Evelyn seemed relieved. I was relieved for a while, too, because they all seemed to leave Roc alone. That was until I saw him and Scorpio outside late last night, talking and standing real close to each other. She kept whispering something in his ear. I wondered what she had said to make such a serious look appear on his face. He kept nodding his head, and when they headed to the bedroom, so did I. I was supposed to sleep in my own room downstairs, but to hell with that. It was scary down there, and more than anything, being down there at night was no fun. The president gave me his bed, while he chilled on the sofa. I hadn't seen him sleep yet, and every time I got up to get me a middle-of-the-night snack, he was still up watching TV, reading or doing a crossword puzzle.

I'd thought it was early, but when I looked at the clock on the wall, it showed nine o'clock in the morning. Everybody's bed was empty, and I looked around, thinking what a mess. Nobody's bed was made, sheets and pillows were on the floor, shoes were strewn here and there and clothes were all over the closet. I called Alex yesterday to see if he would send over a maid service, but nobody had shown up yet. We needed something, because the people in this house, I guess, were used to being waited on. It was no secret that everybody was lazy, even the president who always left his socks in the living room. Every day he rocked a crisp shirt with slacks. Not once had I seen him in a pair of jeans or shorts. Whenever he chilled by the pool, his shirt was off, slacks were still on. Sunglasses shielded his eyes and observing is what he did best. Keith and Roc were hooked up though. Their bodies with all those tats were tight. I couldn't get enough of looking at either of them. That was why I got out of bed, did my duties in the bathroom, got a bowl of Captain Crunch cereal and went to the workout room, where I figured the men would be. When I got there, everybody was there, except the president. I didn't know where he was—his ass was always disappearing. But the loud treadmills were going, the TV was on and grunts from Keith lifting weights could be heard outside the glass door. I opened it, holding the bowl of cereal in my hand.

"Y'all be taking this workout shit too serious for me," I said, looking around at Scorpio on an elliptical machine, Evelyn on a stepper and Chase jogging on a treadmill, next to Roc.

"Yeah, well, you need to get busy too," Roc said. "Put that cereal down and get over here."

"No, thank you. I'll get my workout in later, trust me."

I sat on the floor and started eating my cereal. While I was watching TV, Roc interrupted me again.

"Jada!" he shouted. "Come on, Ma. What in the hell are you doing?"

"Roc, please mind your own business. Don't worry about what I'm doing. Concern yourself with what you doing."

I sipped milk from the bowl, and then I hurried to the kitchen to get two iced cinnamon rolls that were fresh as ever. Icing dripped from the top, and as I went back into the workout room, everybody was looking at me.

"Damn that looks good," Keith said, licking his lips. "Anymore of those left?"

"Yep. But I don't know if it'll be enough for everybody because I already had two last night."

"I had one too," Evelyn said, slowing down on the stepper. "They are good, but I need to finish my exercise before I tackle another one of those."

I bit into the cinnamon roll, licking the icing from my lips. I could see Roc shaking his head, and then he said something to Scorpio that I couldn't hear. She laughed and winked at him. I didn't like that shit one bit, so I spoke up to get his attention away from her, especially since the workout gear she had on had her ass looking even plumper. If I was a man, I'd be trying to fuck her too.

"Roc, you'd better be careful on that treadmill," I warned. "That's the same one I got messed up on. You have to stay real focused on that thing or it will send your ass flying, trust me on this."

Roc was jogging at a fast pace with his muscular calves on full display. His wife- beater was soaked from his sweat, and I had to lick my lips, again, from seeing all that sexy wet blackness.

"You got messed up on here because you didn't know what you were doing. You gotta show this thing some love and use it for its purpose."

Roc started jogging faster, and all of a sudden, the treadmill just stopped. Came to a complete halt, and his ass fell face first. When he bounced on it and hit the floor, I cracked the fuck up! The loud thud caused everybody to shut it down.

Chase got off her equipment to help him. So did Scorpio. "Are you okay?" Chase asked while reaching for his arm to help him off the ground. "That looked painful."

He appeared to be in a daze as Scorpio and Chase helped him to his feet. As he stumbled and attempted to stabilize himself, he shook his head and brushed it off as if everything was all good.

"I'm all right. That . . . That muthafucka just cut off."

"I warned yo ass, didn't I?" I was still laughing hard. "That treadmill don't like black people and it will fight back when you keep pouncing on it like that. You can't get me back on that thing to save my life. I still got scars from when I fell off of it. You, though, need to check those white teeth you got and make sure they're all still there."

Not only was I laughing, but Evelyn and Keith started cackling too. Evelyn laughed so hard that she had to leave the workout room. Realistically, she wasn't fooling anybody. Her ass was on the way to the kitchen to get one of those cinnamon rolls.

Roc looked so embarrassed as he limped away from the treadmill. Scorpio and Chase appeared really concerned about his ass. Their faces were scrunched, and Chase kept asking if he needed some help.

"It looks like your ankle is swelling, Roc. Do you want someone to call a doctor to come here and look at it?"

With a twisted face and eyes squinted, he waved her off while making his way to the door.

"I said I'm good." He spoke in a nasty tone. "I just need to go sit down in the living room and prop my leg up."

"Be careful," Scorpio said. "I'll get you an icepack, and if it looks too bad, Roc, I'm going to request a doctor for you."

Roc didn't respond. He walked out, and the second the door closed, everybody burst into laughter. They had me fooled because I seriously thought they were concerned about his fall. Scorpio was laughing so hard that she was holding her stomach. Chase had dropped back on a weight bench, cracking up. Keith was still at it—the fit of laughter went on for about ten long minutes.

"He hit that muthafucka hard!" I was barely able to catch my breath. "I told him, but he just didn't want to listen. Y'all better stay off that thing. If you're brave enough to get on it, good luck!"

"I'll get on it," Keith said as he walked over to it. "A treadmill is a treadmill, and the only reason Roc fell was because he kept turning his head, talking to you and Scorpio. It didn't have anything to do with the treadmill not liking black people on it."

Keith turned off the treadmill then turned it back on. He started slowly walking on it.

"Men are so stupid," I said, shaking my head. "Y'all don't believe fat meat greasy, and I'm not lying about how that thing feels about black people. You gon' hurt yourself too, but if Scorpio get her mixed, light-bright ass on it, she'll be good."

Scorpio stopped laughing and put her hand on her hip. "Jada, don't even go there, okay? I'm not in the mood to hurt your feelings this morning, so keep eating your cinnamon rolls and shut up. For the last and final time, I am B.L.A.C.K. black."

"The only thing black on you is the hair on your head and pussy. Stop trying to claim something that you ain't."

Chase laughed louder, until Keith chimed in. "No black hair on her pussy for sure."

"Thanks for validating that Keith," Scorpio said, rolling her eyes at me. "I take good care of my shit, and you need to tackle that bushy armpit of yours that's growing pretty wildly."

"I planned on doing it today, but even after it's gone, you still won't be black. With that being said, I gotta go check on my Boo and make sure he's okay. As for you, Keith, I'ma pray for you on that treadmill."

I left the workout area, and as soon as I went inside, I saw Evelyn sitting next to Roc. She had an icepack in her hand and was rubbing it against his ankle that was propped on an ottoman.

"That feels guuuud," he said with his head dropped back, eyes closed. "Damn that feels good."

"I didn't see anything I could wrap your ankle with, but if you put on a sock, it'll keep the icepack in place."

"I don't need all of that," he said. "Just keep massaging it and rubbing that icepack on it." He lifted his head, looking over at me. "Can you get me a couple of aspirin, Jada? My ankle is throbbing just a little. I want to stop the pain before it gets too severe."

"I don't mind getting you any aspirin, but if you're in pain, you need to let me call a doctor."

107

Roc didn't say anything, but that's how men were. He was trying to keep a brave face, but after that fall, I knew something had to be broken. My phone was in the bedroom downstairs. And as soon as I reached the bottom stair, I could hear the president talking. I tiptoed over to a door that led to the storage area in the basement and placed my ear against it. I heard him laugh, and then his voice sounded more serious.

"Maybe in about another week or two," he said. "I don't want anybody to know about this and continue to keep a close eye on my mother." He paused and then he spoke up again. "Keep an eye on her too. If she keeps asking, just say you don't know. I haven't figured out how I'm going to deal with her yet, and I'm still upset about everybody's betrayal. If she hadn't left, we wouldn't be in this predicament." He paused to listen again. But as my dumb ass tried to move in closer to the door, it squeaked. "Let me call you back later."

I rushed away from the door, but by the time I made it to the bedroom, the president called my name. I pivoted, looking like a school girl who had gotten busted for cheating.

"I know we're not supposed to utilize phones while we're in here, but there are important calls I must make every day. Besides, I'm not really interested in winning the million dollars. I'm here for other reasons, if you don't already know."

I nodded and couldn't help it that my thoughts had turned dirty. His voice, his mysteriousness, those lips and his powerfulness . . . all of it turned me on.

"You can use the phone whenever you want to. Who am I to stop you? I didn't hear all of your conversation, but I did hear some of it. I hope everything will be okay with you and the first lady. If not," I cleared my throat and giggled. "You can sleep down here any time, especially since I took over your bed upstairs."

He laughed and crossed his arms. "The first lady and I will be fine, but whenever I need to get some sleep, and whenever I need to step away from everyone, I'll keep that comfortable bed you have in there in mind."

He turned to walk away. As he tackled the stairs, I just shook my head. Some ho's were so lucky and didn't even know it.

I'd called the doctor, and when he got there, he said Roc had a bad sprain. He wrapped his ankle with a stretch bandage and gave him pills for the pain. After the doctor left, I cooked, and for most of the day, we all chilled outside and in the game room. It wasn't until about eight o'clock when we decided to go to the theater room and watch a movie together. The problem was we couldn't agree on what to watch. The men wanted to watch a comedy movie, but the ladies wanted to watch *Fences*, starring Denzel Washington.

"Yes, lawd," Evelyn said. "I've seen every single movie that man has starred in, since *Mo' Better Blues*."

Chase high-fived her. "Me too. I don't care how old he gets or what kind of role he plays, he owns it, doesn't he?"

We all agreed.

"I jumped on his team after *Training Day*," I admitted. "He reminded me of my ex, Kiley, and all that thug stuff going on sold me. I think I've watched that movie about ten or twenty times."

"He definitely deserved an award for that movie," Scorpio said. "And he should have waaay more awards because the man is not only fine, but very brilliant as well. I find myself in a daze while watching his interviews. He's so intelligent, and when those lips move I be like . . . God, help me, please."

Keith cleared his throat. "It would be nice if you ladies would have a seat so we can start checking out this Kevin Hart movie. It's not happening with Denzel tonight, sorry."

"It sure in the hell ain't," Roc said. "So forget it and enjoy the popcorn."

Scorpio looked at the president. "Mr. President, what would you like to watch? A vote will swing this in our favor regardless, but do you care if we watch Denzel or not?"

He sat up straight, wringing his hands together. "I say give the women what they want; therefore, Denzel wins. I heard *Fences* was really a good movie."

Roc and Keith plopped back in their seats, cutting their eyes at all of us. "Man, that's bullshit," Roc said. "I'm cool with Denzel's movies too, but I'd rather be laughing tonight, not crying."

"Yeah, like you cried when you fell off that treadmill," I said, causing everyone to laugh again. "If you want to watch a comedy movie, somebody needs to go get that video from the workout room."

Roc was the only one not laughing. Instead, he jumped up from the chair and threw his bag of popcorn at me. It went everywhere, and after that, I threw my bag at him. Unfortunately, my bag hit the president dead in his face and busted. Buttered popcorn spilled on him too, causing me to cover my mouth with my hand.

"Ooooo, I'm sorry. I didn't mean to do that, sir, Mr. President."

Surprisingly, he fired back at me with his bag. I was being bombarded with popcorn from him, Roc and Keith who was picking up popcorn from the floor, just to throw it at me. I looked at the women who just sat there and giggled.

"Y'all asses better start helping me," I said. "How y'all gon' just sit there and laugh?"

They joined in, and when all was said and done, popcorn and the other snacks we'd brought into the movie room was everywhere. That even included our drinks that rained on our clothes. It was a mess, but as I observed Roc laying over Scorpio, trying to take some pretzels from her hand, I didn't like that shit. There was no breathing room between them, and he was right between her legs as they laughed. Evelyn had her legs wrapped around Keith's back, and as Chase and I double-teamed the president, her ass was all on him. It was becoming clearer to me about who was going to be screwing who. The last thing I wanted was for that bitch Scorpio to get a piece of my Roc. I had to do something about this quick.

Scorpio

I had been having such a good time in Hell House. Not even Jada's insults bothered me anymore, and I started to realize that she often said things just to get attention. That was fine by me. I couldn't care less about her, but what I did care about was the ongoing side-eyeing from Chase that annoyed me from time-to-time. I didn't like how she kept watching my every move. As if she *liked* me or something or she desired to have something that I had. I tried to be nice to her, but every time it seemed as if we were starting to get along, she would flip and say or do something that let me know she had something against me.

Other than her, I was okay. Roc had won me over a little bit, and even though I felt as if he really wasn't on my level, I had to keep in mind that this was how things were today. In no way would he be involved in my future. A man like him didn't fit into my world, and just like Keith, Roc didn't have enough money to get me overly excited about him as a whole. His marital status was another problem. I seriously didn't want to have another woman all worked up over me, so I had to think long and hard about how

I intended to deal with the throbbing in my pussy, every time he stood near me. Every time he playfully wrapped his arms around my waist, whispered something in my ear or just plain ol' carried on a decent and pleasurable conversation with me. He was a smart man, too, and as I started to indulge in many more conversations with him, I started to see a different side to him. He opened up to me about Desa Rae, his children, where he lived and why he'd gone into hiding. Even told me about why he went to jail—his loyalty to friends and family spoke volumes. I was impressed, just not impressed enough. But slowly but surely, that was starting to change.

Evelyn had been all over Keith. I barely had time to follow up on what we'd discussed. He kind of kept his distance from me too, and I wasn't sure if he was actually trying to work through what was going on with him, or if he was upset with me for not having sex with him. He didn't seem like the type who would get upset about something like that, but, sometimes, you just never knew what other people were thinking. Like the president who looked as if he wanted to slap the shit out of me for not voting for him. Then his eyes said something else. I'd caught him looking at me several times, but when I'd look his way he'd turn his head. He was the one person I truly felt was on my level, more so above it. He was my kind of man for sure, and when they came as powerful as he was, his money status, no matter how much it was, could be overlooked.

Thing is, I couldn't figure him out. I didn't know if he was interested in anyone here, and I wasn't about to throw myself at him and get embarrassed. When I went to the movie room that night, my intentions were to kick up a conversation with him, see where his head was at, and find out if he was upset with me for not voting for him. I'd felt kind of bad about it, because he seemed to work real hard at trying to improve things in this country. Unfortunately, I was tired that night and wound up falling asleep. When I woke up, he had laid the blanket over me and was gone. I wasn't sure what time he'd left, but I could have sworn that I felt a gentle kiss on my forehead. Maybe I had been dreaming or tripping for that matter. Nonetheless, there was something about him that intrigued me, more than I was willing to admit.

The one thing I liked to do from time-to-time, and it also helped me forget about some of the things that were going on in my life, was read. While everyone else was either outside or in the living room talking and eating, I stayed in the bedroom reading a good book that had me flipping the pages like crazy. I couldn't even put it down to go to the bathroom. It was that good, and the only interruption that came was when Roc rushed into the room, slamming the door behind him.

"Jada ass is crazy," he said, laughing while trying to catch his breath. "She out there trying to pour some hot ass water on me."

"You must've done something awfully bad to her, didn't you? Because you know Jada is not the kind of woman who will do something like that, just because."

"Like hell," he said then sat on edge of the bed. "What's that you reading?"

I had placed the book on my lap, so I lifted it so he could see the raunchy cover.

"I'm reading a romance novel that is sexy, drama filled and the plot is better than any other plot I've read before."

"It must be one of those novels that be making your panties all sticky and wet. I know all about those, and every time Desa Rae gets finished with one of those books, she be horny as hell. She told me some of those books be better than watching a porn movie."

"I'd have to agree with her. Some of the books I read definitely take me there, but like the one I'm reading now, it's taking me there and offering so much more. As I said, this plot has my mind going in circles. Just when I think something is going to happen, the author shocks me. In addition to that, my panties are getting wet and the couple in this book are on fire."

Roc was blunt, but playful. "Take them off and let me see for myself how wet they are. Not only that, let me read some parts of the book so I can see if it'll be suitable for Desa Rae."

Now, he didn't think I wasn't going to honor his request, did he? I put the book aside, slightly raised my short gown and reached for the string on my thong to remove them. Roc sat in shock as I lifted my butt from the bed and eased down my thong. I tossed it to him; it fell right in his lap.

"Feel free to examine it." My legs remained opened. He had a couple of *things* he could examine.

"I'll take your word for it," he said, removing my thong from his lap and placing it on the bed next to him. He also looked between my legs, and having no shame whatsoever, I opened them even wider, causing him to turn his head. He spoke in a soft tone. "See, you fucking with me now. Don't do that shit, Ma."

I closed my legs and kneeled on the bed, right beside him. My breasts were right at his face; he got a good whiff of my body fragrance that was a sweet heat and spicy. I placed my arms on his shoulders then turned his head to face me.

"Listen, okay," I said. "I'm not trying to take you from your wife, nor do I want you to do anything you'll regret. But with that being said, I'm really feeling you. I wouldn't mind having sex with you, just once, but at your request, not mine. Give it some thought, and let me know what you decide."

After all the joking Roc had done, this time, his facial expression showed seriousness.

"I've heard it all before, Scorpio, and I can recall Chase saying some of that same bullshit to me a while back. But the only person who can take me from my wife is me, not you. I'm the only one who can disrupt my home, and I will give it some thought, but—"

I had to taste his tongue, so I leaned in, placed my mouth over his and went for it. I felt a little resistance, but when his hand slipped between my thighs, I was in business. His tongue started to dance faster with mine, and just as he leaned in to lay me back, he paused. He couldn't say one word, because the door flew open and in walked Jada. Her eyes widened. She held on to the doorknob as she dropped to her knees.

"Mommuuuuh," she cried out while holding her chest. "Momuh, please come back and help me . . . help me get through thiiiiis!"

Her loud voice caused Evelyn and Chase to come see what was up. But by that time, Roc was standing. I was sitting on the bed with my legs crossed.

"What's wrong?" Evelyn said to Jada. "Did something happen to your mother?"

Jada dropped her head back, moving it around as if it was limp and couldn't stay attached to her neck. A tear had even rolled from the corner of her eye. She wiped it.

"My grandmother been gone since the eighties, but I was thinking about her when I came into the room. The memories brought me to my knees. I just couldn't take it."

Roc walked toward the door, shaking his head. "Man, you be tripping sometimes," he said. "You need to quit playing so much."

Jada snapped and frowned as she barked at him. "Naw, nigga, you the one tripping. I'm trying to save your black ass from these thirsty ho's in here, but don't blame me or that crooked dick of yours if you find yourself in trouble again."

He held out his hands, firing right back at her. "I'm all about trouble, Ma. It's whatever."

After he walked out, Chase and Evelyn looked at me. Chase's eyes shifted to my thong on the bed. I happily picked it up, lifted my gown and put it back on. She rolled her eyes and walked out. Evelyn shrugged and did the same. Jada, however, came further into the room, standing next to the bed with her hand on her hip.

119

"You need to be ashamed of yourself. That man is married, Scorpio, and why y'all always gotta be chasing after married men? Y'all must be some real unhappy and lonely bitches. I can't stand homewreckers. First it was Chase, now you."

"Excuse me, Jada, but you can't wreck a home that is already wrecked and damaged in ways that can't be fixed. I don't know what the real deal is with Roc, but whatever we do is really none of your business."

"If it is wrecked, you ain't the one to fix it so go sit your happy ass down somewhere and pass the pussy on to someone other than Roc. Please and thank you."

"Why should I? Because you want you some? Stop griping and go for it, Jada. Good luck and please do watch how you speak to me. I don't appreciate your tone, and I will lay you the hell out, if you keep on saying things and confronting me about shit that is in no way your business."

I was so mad that I got off the bed, snatched up the book I was reading and left the room. Jada mumbled something, but I just kept it moving. She had one more time to disrespect me. Just one more and that was it.

Later that day, things had settled down. We were all in the living room having a good time playing cards, charades and singing karaoke. Many of us had had too much to drink, especially Chase and Keith who had been acting real silly. Roc and Jada were high, and even the president looked as if he had tossed back too many glasses of wine. He said he didn't drink, but I figured that today was an exception.

"Let's play another game," Chase said, scooting to the edge of the sofa, crossing her legs. "It's called, where are they now: the best sex you've ever had."

I didn't have to think long or hard about this—something had already popped into my head. Some looked to be pondering, while others sat around looking as if they were eager to speak up. Jada was the first. She jumped up, rubbing her hands together.

"Oooo, bay-be let me tell y'all how, where and when it all went down! Me and Kiley Jacoby Abrams were in the backseat of his Cadillac. That thing was brand new, and he had just come from the dealership where he threw big dollars on the table and was like . . . I'm taking this with me now. Anyway, before we got home, he pulled over to the curb, hopped in the back and stripped naked. I wasn't moving fast enough, so he yanked me by my hair and pulled me on the backseat with him. After that, it was on! He flipped my legs over his shoulders, rolled me into a ball-like position and started tearing it up. I was screaming and hollering . . . man, that shit was sooooo good. Then, I thought he was coming. But when he pulled out and started shaking his thing, hot piss started shooting everywhere. I rubbed it all over me, as if I was bathing in hot water. Y'all just don't know how good that shit felt. I think I had like four or five orgasms that night. Where is he now? Unfortunately, dead."

Jada moved her head from side-to-side, displaying a sad expression. I just sat there with my mouth wide open. I hoped like hell she was joking, but then again, maybe she wasn't.

"That was too much information, Jada," Evelyn said. "I love sex, but I've never let any man piss on me. What kind of craziness is that?"

"If you ain't tried it," Jada said, bumping her fist with Roc's as he put his up. "You can't knock it."

They laughed and then Roc went on to share his story.

"Mine was on a swing. It was my first time with Desa Rae. The second I entered her, I knew right then I was going to marry her one day. Where is she at right now? Lying in our bed, probably gossiping with her girlfriend, Monica, and missing the hell out of me."

"Awww," Chase said. "How cute? It's so obvious that you've been missing her too."

Roc spoke without hesitating. "Trust me, I am."

I kept my comment to myself, but some men sure did have a funny way of showing how much they *missed* their significant others.

Keith spoke up next. "I can make this real quick," he said. "Mine was on vacation in Mexico with Trina. Hands down, the best sex I've ever had. Period."

"That's because you haven't had me yet," Evelyn said. "Seems like you need a little more experience."

Jada reached over and slapped Evelyn across her back. "Talk about messy, that would be you. How you gon' talk to your best friend's man like that? I wish I had Trina's number so I could call her. She need to remove you from her circle like right now!"

I agreed, but didn't say a word. Keith responded though. "I've had a wealth of experience, and you would hurt yourself trying to teach an old dog new tricks. Evelyn is just talking shit right now. We both know that a move like that would not be in our best interest."

"Speak for yourself," Evelyn said. "I know what's in my best interest. It's just a matter of time before you figure out what's in yours."

Jada added her two-cents, again. "Well, figure it out some other time, because I want to hear what the prez gotta say, if he don't mind saying it."

He placed his hands behind his head, clenching them together. "I . . . I can't really pinpoint who it was, but if I—"

Jada interrupted. "Dang, you been laying pipe to that many women where you can't pinpoint one? That ain't good, Mr. President. Not good at all."

We laughed because I was thinking the same thing. He quickly cleared up what he was trying to say.

"I was saying, if I could decide between *two* people, it would have to be when I was fifteen. It was my first time, and I thought I was so in love with a chick named Teri Bufford. She was fine as ever, and we had sex while her parents were away on vacation. Even though I didn't know what the hell I was doing, she made me feel like our moment together was real special. Today, she's a doctor and she's married to one of my frat brothers from college."

"I was so sure you would mention your wife," Chase said. "But I can understand how your first time would mean a lot to you. It wasn't my first time that took me there, though. I'm not ashamed to admit that I've had multiple safe-sex partners, but the best and most memorable time for me was when I'd had sex with this fine-ass man on the hood of his blue, Aston Martin." She licked across her lips then shifted her eyes to me. "It was spontaneous sex, and as I lay on my stomach and stretched my goodness wide, he worked the hell out of my insides from the back. Kissed my ass, licked my cookies clean . . . I mean, tore me up with a penis that was about this long." She displayed how long it was with her hands. "I couldn't handle all of it, but I came so much that night, I thought I had died and gone to heaven. I'll never forget that look in his gray eyes, and all it took was one, just one orgasm, for me to classify him as the best dick I've ever had. Where is he now? Probably at home with his wife, serving her, exactly what he'd served to me, right after the doors to Hell House closed."

The second Chase had mentioned a blue Aston Martin, I knew exactly where she was venturing to with her story. I narrowed my eyes and listened. Swallowed the lump in my throat and let her finish. When I opened my mouth to speak, Jada opened hers.

"Hell, naw!" she said. "Are you talking about Jaylin Rogers? Did you have sex with him, after everybody was gone?"

"Of course I did," Chase said bluntly. "Who else could I be talking about, other than Scorpio's ex?"

"You mean, Nokea's husband," Jada said. "Y'all need to get that shit right and call a spade a spade. I didn't know y'all had sex, but it shouldn't surprise me one bit. Jaylin done threw that dick all around St. Louis, ain't he?"

"It seems as if he has, Jada," I said sarcastically. "Therefore, no woman should get that excited about a man who has been around, and who probably doesn't even remember one single thing about the night Chase mentioned. Chase, he doesn't even remember your name. And if it did happen, all you were to him was a piece of available ass, nothing more, but a whole lot less."

Chase laughed then pursed her lips. "If I had a phone, I would call him so he could tell you how true it is. So he could let you know how much he does remember me, and even if I was a piece of ass, he would tell you that it was a damn good piece of ass."

Jada whipped out a phone from her pocket. "Start dialing. Somebody give me the digits so I can call him right now."

I looked at Chase. "Give her the number, Chase. Since you know him so well, and sex with you was all that, I'm sure you should have his number, don't you?"

"Unfortunately, his number is in *my* phone. I don't have it with me right now."

"Sure," I said, snatching the phone from Jada's hand. "When it's so good to you, and you've been more than good to him, you'd be able to call like this and get an instant reply."

126

I punched in Jaylin's phone number and hit the speakerphone button. The room was so quiet, you could hear a pin drop. On the second ring, he answered.

"Jaylin Rogers."

"Scorpio Valentino. Are you busy?"

"Somewhat, but what's up?"

"I'm sitting here with an old friend of yours. She just said some interesting things about you, but the one thing that caught my attention was what she said about you and her having sex on the hood of your car." I paused for him to say something, but he didn't respond. "Do you know what friend I'm talking about?"

He finally spoke up. "Scorpio, don't call me with this dumb shit. Is there anything else you wanted?"

"Chase. Her name is Chase Jenkins. Do you know her? Apparently, she thinks she knows you. Well."

"Fuck Chase, and find somebody else to talk about tonight, other than me. I don't know shit about having sex on the hood of my car, and if that's what you really called to ask me, it's time for you to question the dial tone."

I pushed, just to be clear. "I figured you didn't know her, or you just don't remember her like she thinks you do."

"Well, his ass better remember me," Jada shouted into the phone. "Hi, Jaylin! It's me, Jada. Whutzzz up, my nigga?"

We all heard dead silence. After that, Jaylin was no more.

"His battery must've went out on that cheap ass phone he got," Jada said. "Dial him again so I can holla at him."

I deleted his number from Jada's call log then tossed the phone back to her. "If you hit redial, do so at your own risk," I said then looked at Chase. "My story would've been a whole lot better than yours, and, at least, the man I titled as being my best lover knows me and knows me well. Good night, bitch, see you in the morning."

I left the room feeling as if one of us was going to have to leave here soon, before somebody got seriously hurt. It definitely wasn't going to be me.

Roc

Scorpio was a trip. But she almost caused me to slip, fall and bump my head. I don't know why, but the temptation around this muthafucka was real. So real that I felt a need to keep my distance. That was what I always did when I found myself in these situations, and after I'd fucked up the last time, I kept telling myself that it would never happen again. As a matter of fact, I promised myself that it wouldn't.

While the women were inside, Keith, me and the prez were outside shooting hoops. We didn't have a game going—just shooting the ball and talking shit about all that had been going on. For me, this time Hell House felt different. There was chaos, but chaos that didn't linger. We could say something foul to each other one minute; the next minute shit was all good. The only two who seemed not to get along well were Chase and Scorpio. Even so, they still kept their arguments to a minimal and quickly put their differences aside.

Maybe because we all knew that Alex was coming back soon to tell us who *they* decided *they* wanted to leave the house. I wasn't sure if it was time for me to go yet, but like the last time, I always played to win. I wanted to win for sure, and if winning meant I had to stay here and fight off the temptation, I would.

"Unfortunately," Keith said, chest-passing the ball to me. "I've seen some changes in Evelyn and I've given some consideration to her suggestion about us hooking up. I know it's a dangerous move with Trina being her best friend, but why do I feel as if Trina wouldn't care at all? It would be her way of finally getting rid of me."

Keith had given us a lot of background on his situation with Trina. To me, it didn't seem like she really cared for the brother, but I wasn't so sure if fucking around with her best friend was going to help his situation improve.

"I'm not a fan of the Trina you've been talking about, man, and there are always two sides to every story. But if after all this time, she's still confused about who she wants to be with, it's time to jet. If you start hooking up with Evelyn, it would be seen as revenge and revenge only. I think you're looking for a way to get Trina back for all she's done. Evelyn seems to be a person that you know for a fact will stick it to Trina and get her where it hurts."

"I agree with most of that," the prez said. "And revenge is exactly what you seem to be seeking. But don't travel down that path. You will only hurt yourself. Since there is a child involved, you really need to have a serious conversation with Trina about how you feel. If the two of you can't work it out, just let it go. Find someone who is in no way connected to Trina and give that woman the love you have to offer. From what you've said, I can flat-out say that Trina doesn't appreciate you. She may love you in her own little way, but it doesn't seem as if the love she's been representing is enough."

"I assure you it's not," Keith responded as he bounced the ball. He took a shot and missed. I reached up to get the ball, tucking it underneath my arm and listening to Keith continue. "I've been making some plans to move on, but then I keep asking myself if I'm moving on, what harm would one or two nights of sex with Evelyn cause? Trina would be mad, but at this point, I'm starting not to care about how she feels anymore."

I shrugged and continued to tell him how I felt about the shit.

"From what you told us about Evelyn, she doesn't seem like the kind of chick who would be down with one or two nights. She would want more, and I'm telling you that she seems like the kind of chick who would have you living with many regrets. Keep in mind that any woman who keeps on fucking over friends . . . something ain't right with her. I mean, where is the loyalty at?"

Keith nodded and looked at the prez. "So, what did you decide about you and the first lady? She's been doing some messed up things too, but you can't keep having sex with other women, just to make her pay for her actions. I never believe what the media says, but since you told us what's true and what's not, it seems like you have to find a solution for your marriage soon."

I passed the ball to the prez. He bounced it up and down while in thought. He took the ball to the hoop, but missed.

"Unlike some people," he said. "I try not to get hung up on this sex thing too much. Many people will disagree with me, but I firmly believe that when you're severely unhappy at home, and you've done everything you can to try and fix your problems, sex with someone else isn't a big deal. The first lady has shown a lack of effort when it comes to us fixing our problems. I've spoken to her until I'm blue in the face, and the most difficult thing for me to accept is her lies. They just keep on coming. Then she cries, says she's sorry, begs for forgiveness, and I'm supposed to pretend that everything is okay and forgive her. Then, when I meet someone and have sex with them, the world views me as a dog who can't control himself. It's crazy. The most hurtful thing that I may be forced to do is get a divorce. It only makes sense for us, but with me being the president, I question what kind of message our divorce would send to the world, especially about African American couples."

"The wrong message," Keith said. "But your happiness is what's important. Besides, you really have to have your head on straight while running this country. If you have a woman who doesn't have your back, what else can you do but call it quits?"

"I gotta agree," I said, sitting on the bench while tying my tennis shoes. "Sometimes, when I see you on TV and shit, I be thinking about how unhappy you look. I know you gotta deal with world problems, but the least you can do is have a woman at home who got her shit together. There is only so much talking a couple can do, and fuck what people think. To hell with how they feel. Women don't understand our struggles, and the first thing they want to do is point their fingers and talk about how no good we are. I've seen, read and heard about some of the shit the first lady has done. Desa Rae be like . . . *she's so sweet and her husband ain't shit. I feel so sorry for her, and why would he cheat on her like that?* I be like what, Ma? We on the outside looking in. That man trying to run a country and his wife up in a hotel room with secret service, talking about her feelings hurt. Not to mention that she left yo ass in the midst of some serious storms. I can't really say what you should do, but a little extra sex never hurt nobody, with the exception of me."

We all laughed, before heading to the game room to play pool. That was where I elaborated more on my situation with Scorpio, since Keith had asked.

"She's been fucking with me, so I'ma continue fucking with her. The flesh is, no doubt, weak, and the struggle to stay committed, for some, is real. But all it takes is for me to step back for a minute and think about all the shit me and Desa Rae went through to be together. I fought hard to be with her, and after my many bad decisions, she had some tough decisions to make about staying with me. I can't keep taking advantage of her, and I promise y'all that I won't. Scorpio's pussy gon' have to be handed to the next man, and as good as that shit looks, that man will not be me."

"I concur," Keith said. "It does look good."

"Looks can be very deceiving, and what looks good may very well not be good for you," the prez added.

We all agreed.

Chase

I wasn't good at pretending, but I did. I pretended that I wasn't starting to hate Scorpio as much as I did, and something inside of me was building fast. So fast that I couldn't stop it. Every time I looked at her my flesh crawled. I cringed and had visions of me beating the shit out of her, choking her and even killing her. I watched her as she slept. Paid attention to her every move and rolled my eyes at her, every time I got a chance. I kept asking myself why my hate had grown so strong. For one, she was not likeable at all. We had to listen to all she had and how wealthy she was. About her ex-husband who was worth billions, to how much her baby daddy, Jaylin, had done for her and their kids. She wasn't nothing but a gold-digging tramp who had used her good looks and ass to get to where she was. She was the worst of the worst when it came to women, and there was no other way for me to put it.

Then, on top of that, she started going after Roc. I didn't trip when she started leading Keith on—he wasn't nothing but a puppet. But to go after Roc the way she did was the last straw.

She proved to me what kind of woman she was. Yes, I'd pursued him in the past, but there was a reason behind why I did what I did. I wanted payback for my sister who I felt had turned her back on me for many years. I was still somewhat bitter about that, but it wasn't a big issue for me now. This thing between Roc and Scorpio was. He was a damn dog, and who in the hell did he think he was, playing these games, again, and believing that my sister would continue to put up with his shit? Lord knows I wanted to call her. Just to say hello, and to tell her to come get this happy dick fucker who obviously did what the hell he wanted to do. I despised men like him, and in my opinion, Roc wasn't nothing but a young, thug-ass fool who needed his world to be turned upside down. Desa Rae could do so much better than this. She deserved better, but some women were so damn stupid that any man would do. Any man whatsoever, and I bet if I'd had Desa Rae's number to call and tell her about this, she would laugh at me and call me a liar.

On the flipside to my madness, the president and I had been talking a lot. Out of everyone here, he was the one I connected with the most. He was a smart man, but unfortunately, he was another man married to a needy, dumb bitch who couldn't get her act together.

See, a lot of these problems stemmed from men looking for dime pieces to have for show, instead of finding women who had their backs. They ran from the good women, only to hook up with airhead ho's who wasn't good at nothing but sucking dick. They probably weren't even good at that, but they looked good on the men's arms. And by making decisions to be with somebody based solely on their looks, the men paid the price. I mean, these bitches couldn't even cook. Couldn't even prepare a meal and feed their men. I could cook my ass off, but I refused to do so up in here. Nobody in here paid my bills, gave me good loving or had my back. Therefore, Jada would be responsible for doing what she did best. That was running her loud mouth, mispronouncing shit, cooking and eating. She definitely didn't have it all together, but to me, she had more to offer than the first lady. She had more to offer than that trick Scorpio, and what kind of man wanted to be with Evelyn's backstabbing ass? Keith was a fool. I'd lost respect for him when I'd found out more about his current situation. Being fine as fuck just wasn't good enough for me anymore. Like it or not, this shit was the truth.

Roc and Scorpio were at it again—this time in the swimming pool. I sat in the lounging chair, taking peeks at them from behind my dark sunglasses. The fire-red bikini I had on was banging, but I guess it didn't compare to the black one Scorpio had on that had everything hanging out, once again. Jada had on a one piece swimming suit with a wrap around her waist. A floppy hat to block the sun was on her head, and she was on the other side of the pool area, talking to the president who had on slacks. His shirt was off—boy was he hooked up right. Him and Jada were doing a whole lot of serious talking. I couldn't help but to wonder if her breath stunk the way she kept blowing it on him. I wasn't sure where Keith and Evelyn were. I'd seen them feeling each other up the other night, and when I came outside to pretend as if I was looking for something, they quickly separated from each other. Right then, I knew something was up, and shame, shame, shame on it all!

Scorpio was supposed to be playing volleyball with Roc, so it wasn't even necessary for her to have her body pressed against his and giggling so much. I wondered how Jaylin could have two kids by this heifer, and my respect for him had gone down a few notches. I wasn't sure if he remembered what had happened between us or not, but he probably said what he'd said to Scorpio because his wife was somewhere close. It didn't matter to me anyway. Like I'd said . . . he wasn't paying my bills so to hell with him and to his nasty dick that really had been good to me in every way. I chuckled, laughing about what I'd been thinking.

"Rocky Dawson, you'd better stop cheating," Scorpio said, falling all over Roc. "There are consequences for not playing fair, and if you lose, my brotha, you just lose."

"I don't have to cheat to win," he said. When he lifted her and threw her a few feet away from him, I'd seen enough. "Now, go to your side and start over."

Scorpio kicked her legs while screaming and laughing. *Bitch, bitch, bitch, I thought. What a bitch?* I took a few more sips from the Strawberry Daiquiri I'd been drinking, and then I went inside to go handle something I'd been working on. I checked my surroundings, before heading downstairs to the basement. I quietly made my way to a storage room, opening the door to go inside. There was a blanket I had used to cover up some of the things I'd put together, and underneath the blanket was a red container of gasoline and matches. There was also bottled water, for me, some extra pieces of clothing, for me, and several hundred dollars I had taken from Jada's wallet. I wasn't sure where her broke ass had gotten the money from, but I took it because I was sure I would need as much money as I could get, when I set this damn house on fire and watch all of these backstabbing, dick happy, and slutty ho's burn in hell. The only person I didn't want to hurt was the president. But since he was here, I really didn't have a choice. He'd have to burn too, and I would walk away from this feeling real good about doing away with people who had hurt so many others too many times.

I added a few more dollars to my hidden stash, but when I heard a loud moan, I backed away from the covered pile then closed the door to the storage room. The moans got louder and louder, and as I tiptoed to the bedroom area where Jada was supposed to sleep, I saw that the door was closed. I kind of knew what was up, but it wasn't until I cracked the door and looked inside when everything was confirmed. Evelyn and Keith were having sex. She was riding him while his hands were gripped on her ass. I watched lustfully as he slowly guided her up and down on his glazed black dick. She moaned, every time she'd made a soft landing on his lap. Her curves from the backside looked nice, and when he released her ass, his hands traced her curves to help calm her grunts and moans that said his dick must've been too much for her to handle.

"Keeeeith," she whined. "How does it feel, baby? Do you like this? Tell me you're enjoying yourself. Pleeease."

"I am, daaamn, yes, I am."

Right then, he moved her off of him and positioned her on her back. While kneeling over her face, he tapped her mouth with the tip of his head, signaling for her to open it. As she did, she sucked on his pipe, moaning some more. His ass tightened as he forced speedy thrusts into her mouth, and by now, I was getting kind of hot and bothered from watching them. I cuffed my hand over my pussy and started to rub my pearl. As Keith rubbed all over Evelyn's fake, wobbling titties, I envisioned him touching mine. His hand lowered to her coochie, and as his fingers slipped inside of her, she kept opening her legs wider then closing them. He definitely had her on the brink of an orgasm, but what sent me into overdrive was when he sprayed her mouth with his juices. Keith damn near knocked out her teeth—he was moving so fast. Evelyn couldn't keep up, and I got mad watching her lack of skills. So mad that I gave my pearl some relief and dropped my hands by my sides. I opened the door wider, and when they saw me, they both jumped again. Keith backed a few inches away from Evelyn. She sat up, reaching for the sheet to cover herself.

"I am so sorry for interrupting," I said with wide eyes. "I thought I heard someone in here crying. I came to see who it was. I didn't mean to bust in here like this, but please continue and pay me no mind."

"We . . . We were almost done anyway," Keith said. "Sorry for the noise."

"Hey, no problem. But if you want to make *more* noise, I can kind of help out with that."

Keith stared at me, I stared at him. I knew he was down, but when my eyes shifted to Evelyn, she had a look like . . . hell no.

"You may as well leave," she said. "I don't get down like that, and you really did interrupt at the wrong time."

I looked at Keith again—he didn't say one word. I read him so well, and as I started to remove my clothes, the look in his eyes said it all.

"There's a first time for everything, Evelyn," I said. "Either join us or get the fuck out."

She snatched up the sheet, covered her whole body with it and chose to leave. But before she exited, she turned to look at Keith.

"I don't see you exiting," she said. "Surely, you don't want to go there, right?"

He looked at me lying on the bed with my legs wide open, waiting to receive him. I tossed him a condom that was on the nightstand, and without even answering Evelyn, he opened the package with his two front teeth. She stormed out of the room. I laid there with my legs wrapped around Keith's back, having the time of my life.

Evelyn

I was too mad. Mad as hell to be exact, and who did Chase think she was, coming in on us like that, taking over. Women would always be women, but what Keith did was unforgiveable. It was disrespectful in so many ways, and I didn't even want to ever look at him again. I regretted going there with him, but every day we had been in this house, he kept making passes at me and saying things that he knew would get me stirred up. I'd said some things too, but this was downright ridiculous. Talk about feeling dissed—I surely felt that way. I wasn't willing to stay here another day, so I headed to the bedroom, hurrying to put on some clothes so I could go.

The Hell House rule book said that we could leave at any time, without reason. I didn't care about winning the money anymore, even though I needed it. Life had been good, just not great. I'd been going from one job to the next, but the last job I had been at for almost eight months. All it did was pay my bills. It was time to get back to it, because this shit wasn't worth it. I wasn't sure if I would ever tell Trina about what had happened between me and Keith, but I was too embarrassed right now to even think about it. If she actually married his ass, I would say something. But marriage was a long way off between the two of them. That I was sure of.

It took me ten or fifteen minutes to pack my belongings, and if anything was left, I surely didn't care. I marched out of the bedroom with my luggage in tow. Hoped like hell I didn't see Chase or Keith, but when I stepped into the living room area, Jada was sitting on the sofa, eating an apple. The crunch was loud and she was smacking hard. She glanced at my luggage then turned her head back toward the TV.

"This apple is so juicy and good. Since everybody been working out, and I haven't been doing nothing, the least I can do is try to eat right. I'm planning on making baked, pineapple chicken and grilled asparagus tonight. But it looks like you won't be here to enjoy it."

"Unfortunately not. I need to call a cab to come get me, so if you have a phone I could use that would be great."

"I do have a phone, but tell me why you leaving. It wouldn't have anything to do with the fuck room downstairs, would it?"

"What's the fuck room?"

"The room you were just fucking in, and the same one Chase and Keith are screwing in now. Roc and Scorpio than fucked in there too, and if they go there again, I just may join them."

Scorpio came inside, and when I looked at her, she had a frown on her face. "What did you say, Jada? I've been where?"

"Too close to Roc, but gone somewhere. Evelyn and me talking."

Scorpio threw her hand back and went to the bathroom. I wasn't sure if Jada had told the truth or not about Roc and Scorpio, but it bothered me that she knew what Keith and I had been doing.

"How do you know what Keith and I were doing?"

"Because there are cameras all over this place, especially in the bedrooms. I don't know why y'all be trying to be slick. We told y'all this stuff may be shown on TV. I mean, we can only cut so much. How do you think Trina gon' feel when she may see you screwing her damn man?"

"First of all, it was communicated to me that we all have to agree to what is shown on TV. If we didn't agree, it wouldn't be shown. I'm not agreeing to anything, and I'm getting out of here today."

"You can do what you want to, but stop being so silly. This show is about making money, as are most reality shows. Do you think for one minute the show producers will let you tell them what they can and cannot put on TV? They will find the most outrageous shit to put on there; shit that makes them money. Their objective is to get paid, and a broke bitch like you ain't got no pull to stop them from doing what they want to do."

"For your information, I'm not broke. I will also sue, so you can tell them that, when you talk to them."

"Sue with what? Your looks? I don't think so, Evelyn, besides, you ain't really all that. You just gon' have to hold your breath and hope that things work out in your favor. If they don't, just remember that you put your own self in this situation. Goodbye, and you can wait by the front door for your cab to arrive. It will be here soon."

I had nothing else to say, but the producers of Hell House didn't want to fuck with me. I would get the money to sue them, and I wanted every single video with me in it erased.

Mr. President

Things around here had started to get sticky. But from what I could see, as well as sense, something wasn't right. As I had always done, I befriended people, just not to judge them by what was on paper, but by what I exactly saw for myself. How they acted and responded to certain things was important, and you could always tell certain things about a person by simply having a conversation with them. That was what I'd done with everybody, and I didn't like what one person in particular had been doing. She thought she was being slick, and she was able to get away with a whole lot of things because no one had been paying attention. I mean, we'd had some interesting days and nights here already. I enjoyed playing games, watching TV, eating our hearts out, exercising, swimming . . . all of that. I hated to put an end to the fun, but I felt as if it was coming sooner than expected.

It was almost midnight and everyone was still wide awake, partying hard outside. The music was loud, alcoholic beverages were being passed around and a Soul Train line had been going on for ten or so minutes. One by one, we danced down the aisle, clowning and showing what we were made of. Even I had to go back to the days when myself and my frat brothers used to do our thing, and it just so happened that Keith was an Omega Psi Phi Que too. Roc wasn't, but that didn't stop him from joining in with us to chant and *stomp the yard*. The women were meowing and barking right along with us.

"At least I know who can *really* turn up the heat in the bedroom now," Jada said. "You can always tell what's up with a man by the way he dances. You can tell what's up with women too. And all y'all bitches need to sit down because crowd pleasers y'all are not. Too much stiffness going on up in here!"

Scorpio turned her ass to Jada, presenting what she had been working with. When Jada slapped her ass real hard, Scorpio got upset and the party was now over.

"Don't put your hands on me like that again," she said with a frown on her face. "This ass is made for men to smack, not women."

"Then don't push that stanky muthafucka up on me again. Flaunt that shit elsewhere and stop putting it on people with your nasty self."

They went on and on for about an hour. By then, mostly everyone had gone to the bedroom and called it a night. I remained in the living room, meditating with my eyes closed. My head was tilted back; my mind was focused. I had been in my zone for, at least, thirty minutes, and when I opened my eyes I took a long, deep breath. I stood and stretched, before I tackled the stairs to go to the basement. A cigarette was in my pocket. After all that had transpired at the White House, I'd started to smoke every now and then. I put the cigarette in the corner of my mouth, and when I opened the door to the storage room, that was when I saw Chase. She stood, looking like a deer in headlights. I leaned against the doorway with the cigarette still dangling from my mouth. One of my hands was dipped into the pocket of my slacks, and with no shirt on, I knew Chase was surprised to see me.

"Wha . . . Hello, Mr. President," she said with a smile. "What are you doing down here?"

I removed the cigarette from my mouth. Much seriousness was trapped in my eyes. "The question is, what are you doing down here? Shouldn't you be upstairs sleeping?"

"I should, but I couldn't sleep. I came down here to see if I could find some more blankets because I got real cold. Someone mentioned that the storage room had some extra blankets, so I thought I'd find one." She lustfully examined me with her sneaky, narrowed eyes. "When I find a blanket, would you like to go into the room over there and get cozy with me?"

I turned my head to look toward the room. "Are you talking about that room over there? The room where you just had sex with Keith?"

She didn't hesitate to answer. "Yes, the room where I had sex with Keith, and the room where you and I *will* have sex too."

I chuckled and faced her again. "I love confident women, Chase, really I do. I think women are special, and this world is undeniably a better place because of all of you. But the kind of women I despise are jealous, spiteful, revengeful and hateful women who are masterful at manipulating men, and who get mad when things don't go according to their plans. You know the ones who plot all the time and do cruel shit that turn people's world upside down. Those women, no, women and men both, anger me to my core. Every time I come across one of those people, who remind me of terrorists, it triggers something inside of me. As president, I do snap, and when I do, the end result is not always pretty."

Chase swallowed and continued with her manipulation. "Well, when the president snaps, I think I may have a cure."

"Trust me, you don't. But what you do have are some matches over there so I can light my cigarette. Why don't you get me a match, alright? I really need it right now, because if I don't get my fix, something tragic may happen."

Chase saw the look in my eyes. She knew that this was no laughing matter. She was well aware that I'd known about her plan to burn all of us up in this motherfucking house tonight, and try to walk out of here as if she had done nothing. Man or woman, that was cold. What she was to me was evil. Evil people didn't deserve a place in my world, and so as long as I was the president, they wouldn't.

"I . . . There are no matches here, sorry," she said, appearing brave and fearful at the same time. The look was in her eyes.

"Yes, there are some in here. Right underneath that blanket, next to the container of gasoline."

She bent over to remove the blanket. And right when my eyes shifted to it, she made an attempt to rush out of the storage room. She didn't get far. I grabbed her neck, shoving her ass back. She stumbled to keep her balance.

"Wha . . . What in the hell are you doing?" she shouted. "Don't put your damn hands on me! I don't care who you are!"

I definitely didn't want her to wake the others with her loud voice, so I prepared myself to quickly put an end to this. I snatched up the container of gasoline, dousing her with it as she backed into a corner, starting to yell even louder.

"Are you fucking crazy!" she hollered. "Don't put that shit on me! Stop it!"

I dropped the container then snatched up the matches. Chase's eyes got real wide.

"I'm not crazy, Chase, but you definitely are. And then some."

Instead of striking a match, I reached for her arm and pulled her out of the room. Her body quivered, but she thought shit was all good because I didn't strike the match. What I did was shove her against a concrete wall and clamp my hands tightly around her neck. I squeezed tighter and tighter, lifting her feet from the ground and looking into the eyes of what I considered to be one of the devil's many children. She scratched at my hands for a while, but soon, her arms dropped by her sides. Her lips trembled, but stopped. Eyes then closed. I slowly released my hands, and as I removed them from her neck, her limp body dropped to the floor. I stepped away from it then reached for the phone in my pocket. When I heard his voice, he already knew what to do.

"Pick her up, dispose of her body and do it before the others wake up."

That was all I'd said, before walking up the stairs and closing the door behind me. I went outside, flicking the cigarette away—I felt as if I didn't need it anymore. All I'd thought about was, it was my job to protect the American people. All Americans, whether they had issues or wasn't living their lives like other people expected. Chase wasn't about to let no bullshit like that happen on my watch, and she had certainly underestimated me. As president, sometimes, I had a reputation to uphold on the outside. On the inside, well, I was a motherfucker.

I washed my hands . . . cleaned myself up a bit and then went into the theater room where I'd told Scorpio to meet me around two in the morning. To no surprise, she was there. She turned her head when the door opened, smiling at me.

"You asked me to be here, but I almost thought you weren't going to show up. I didn't see you on the sofa; I had no idea where you'd gone."

I sat next to her, calmly crossing one leg over the other. My hands were clenched together behind my head; I took a quick glance at the movie screen where a comedy movie was playing.

"I'm always disappearing and doing things I probably have no business doing in here. I can only do those things while Jada is sleeping—you know she's like the police around here. I had some private phone calls to make, so I went to the side of the house to make them."

"So, in other words, you broke the rules."

I placed my finger over my lips. "Shhhh, don't tell. That's just between us."

"Just like this is between us, right?"

Scorpio leaned in, placing her lips over mine. Our tongues connected—the taste was real sweet, as I'd expected it to be. She paused to back away from me, and when she did, she lifted her nightgown over her head. She then straddled my lap, and as the reclining chair fell back, I closed my eyes, allowing her to have her way with me, like I knew she would make every attempt to do. My immediate thought was, the world would never be the same, as long as I was the president.

Jada

Chase had booked up! In the middle of the night, she had gotten the hell out of here and nobody had seen her since. I wasn't so sure what had pissed her off to make her want to leave, but that could have been a number of things. Her and Evelyn were cowards. They could dish it out, but damn sure couldn't take it. I was glad they were gone, and for the past three days, things had been real peaceful. I started to feel better too, especially since Scorpio had seemed to back off Roc a little. He hadn't been paying her that much attention either, but now her trifling self seemed to be getting too close to the president. He honestly didn't seem that interested in her, but when it came to men, nobody knew what they were thinking. I just didn't think a man like him would stoop that low, even though Scorpio was not as bad as Chase was.

If my calculations were correct, Chase had screwed Roc, Jaylin and Keith. The only reason Prince didn't get none last time was because he'd been booted out too soon. The only other man she hadn't gotten a piece of was the president, but then again, she probably had. I couldn't believe how trifling she was. That was just too much dick for one woman to handle. At some point a bitch had to say enough is enough. Maybe, just maybe, she left to reflect on the consequences of being a ho.

While the men sat around watching football games, Scorpio and I were in the kitchen.

"Jada," she said, bending over the island. "When you get time, I want you to tell me your favorite dish and show me how to cook it. Will you do that for me?"

"I can show you how *I* would cook it, but when your hands start touching everything, it doesn't mean the dish will turn out the same way."

"Maybe not, but let's give it a try. You've been cooking some dishes that I be in bed dreaming about. I'm dead serious too. Even my housemaid, Loretta, don't be throwing down like you. I may have to pay you to come to my house and work for me."

"I don't want to do that kind of work for a living, but how much would you be willing to pay me, do you have any pets, are your kids pests and will I get to see Jaylin? I tried to call him back the other night, but he blocked my damn number. He's a silly muthafucka. I don't know how in the world you deal with him."

Scorpio laughed. "What I would pay you would surprise you, I don't have any pets and my children are the most awesome kids ever. As for Jay Baby, he is so misunderstood. He got all that bark and very little bite. He's extremely loving, and if he truly cares about you, I mean, you can have it all."

"I'm talking about Jaylin Rogers, bitch. I don't know what Jaylin you talking about, but the one who was here last time was a hot ass mess. He did come through for me, though. I guess he got some good qualities, but not enough for me to be married or involved with a man like that. He got that control thing going on, and in my world, a man ain't about to control nothing. I be like go sit yo ass down somewhere cause I got this right here. All of it and thank you very much for trying to assist me."

Scorpio laughed, and when I told her lasagna was my favorite dish, she asked me the best way to make it. Just as I got ready to show her the ropes, the doorbell rang. I was surprised because Alex said he wasn't stopping by until next Wednesday. I didn't think it was him, but as everyone looked at me, I quickly spoke up.

"Not many people know we're here, but it's probably the maid service. I'll be right back."

The president stood. "I'll go get it. Why don't you finish doing what you were doing and let me go see who it is?"

"Nope, because the rules say you're not allowed to do that. I can handle opening the door, so sit down and keep watching the game."

He sat back down and I headed to the door. When I opened it, I took several steps back, my mouth hung wide open.

"You must be at the wrong house," I said to the most gorgeous looking Italian man I'd ever seen. He reminded me so much of Halle Berry's ex-husband, and all I could think about was his naked, sexy ass in the movie *Unfaithful* that we had just watched the other night in the theater room. Fine hair was on his face, his skin looked real rich and smooth, and the clothes he had on damn sure didn't come from a mall.

"I'm looking for Scorpio Pezzano. Is she here?"

I cocked my head back and squinted. "You ain't Mario, are you?"

"Yes. Is she here?"

His attitude was a little snobby. I didn't want to go off on his ass. I started not to let him inside, but since Scorpio was on my good side today, what the hell?

"She in here, but she told us her name is Scorpio Valentino. I don't know about all this Pizza . . . Pezzani stuff."

"Pezzano," he said, correcting me as he stepped inside.

I ignored him correcting me, and if he said one more thing I didn't appreciate, I was gon' have to go off on his stuffy ass.

I directed him down the hallway, and as I walked behind him, all I could think about was why some bitches were so lucky. Maybe I needed to start dating again. I had been so afraid to open up and give somebody a real chance, ever since Kiley and me parted ways. I'd dated here and there, but I kept thinking about all the love I'd had for Kiley. It wasn't as if our relationship was all that, but that nigga took good care of me. Real good care, and I ain't had nobody . . . nobody who looked out for me as much as he had. More than anything, he accepted me as is. Then again, we did use to fight a lot, and I got upset when I'd thought about a fight we'd had. He punched me in my face. Maybe I was better off without him.

When Mario stepped into the living room area, all eyes were on him. He didn't say shit to nobody—his eyes were focused on Scorpio. The expression on her face was flat. She didn't appear happy to see him at all.

He held out his hand to hers. "I want you to come home with me, now. Stop all of this nonsense, babe, and move back in with me. I've given you enough time to think about us. I'm not going to wait any longer."

"Listen," I had to say. "If she won't move back in with you, I most certainly will. I got some of my clothes in that closet back there, and the rest of that shit can stay at my house. Think long and real hard about this . . . please."

Of course, my offer was ignored. Damn.

"Jada, you can start packing because I'm not going anywhere with him. I don't even know why you're here, Mario, and who are you to show up here like this?"

"I'm a man who still loves you very much. I made some mistakes and I'm sorry. Sorry for everything. I promise you Camila and our baby won't interfere."

I pretended to play a violin while humming through the bullshit. Some men needed to get it the fuck together. All this sorry mess was for the birds.

"Blah, blah, blah," Scorpio said and rolled her eyes. "You're wasting your time and your breath. I've been sooo good without you. There is no way that I'm going to go back to living in hell with you."

Mario released a deep sigh. He finally took a moment to look at all three men on the sofa, staring at him. They were probably thinking what a pitiful looking motherfucker, but I was sure all of them had been in similar situations like this before.

Mario dropped his hand, looking at Scorpio again. "Please," he said. "Just one more chance. One more, and if I ever screw up again, you can strip me of everything. You can have it all, babe. All of it, cause all I want right now is you."

Okay. Now he was talking my language. I had to talk some sense into Scorpio. She was tripping.

"Girl, do you need me to go get your things? He said you can have *all* of it. And by the looks of it, he got a lot of *it*. Besides, most men ain't nothing but a bunch of cheating, no good, low down, sneaky, dirty ass, lying, conniving—"

Mario swung around, looking at me with a twisted face. "Would you please shut the fuck up? Damn, man, you need to zip it!"

I tightened my fist and swung at his ass. Luckily he ducked, and by then, Roc had gotten up to back me away from Mario.

"Damn, Ma, calm down," Roc said as he held me back. "Yo ass be tripping."

"Scorpio, you'd better give this sucker an answer and get him out of here before I whup his ass! He don't know me to be talking to me like that. I don't care how much money he got—yo money don't mean nothing up in here."

Scorpio had already stepped up to Mario, and as he grabbed her waist, I saw her look at the president from the corner of her eye. He slowly moved his head from side-to-side. I didn't know what in the hell that meant, but it caused her to back away from Mario and tell him to leave.

"You're making a fool of yourself," she said. "I'll call you whenever I get home so we can talk, but please do not expect to hear good news."

"I'm going to keep hope alive."

He tried to kiss her, but she backed up and glanced at the president again. I was stunned. *Had they been fucking and I didn't know about it?* I had some investigating to do, but for now, I had to make sure Mario got out of here. Five minutes later, he was gone. Scorpio seemed so upset that she went outside to gather herself. The fellas got back to the game and for the next few hours they were occupied. I cooked dinner, but every now and then I glanced at the president, especially when Scorpio had come inside and went to the bedroom. He didn't look her way, but my eyes knew what they had seen. There I was thinking that her and Roc had been hooking up. My Boo hadn't done a thing. He was good or, at least, I hoped he was. I would surely find out soon, and when everybody went to sleep tonight, I had some digging to do.

Later that night, I went to my bedroom downstairs. It had been cleaned up by the maid service, but I wasn't about to sit on the bed because I knew Keith's ol' nasty self had leaked his juices on it. So had Chase, as well as Evelyn. I wondered what the two of them had been doing since they'd left here, and as I sat at the desk, starting to watch some of the videos that had been filming everyone here, I laughed at some of the things I saw. I pursed my lips, rolled my eyes and even gagged. Nothing really shocked me, until I saw Scorpio go into the theater room. The president went in after her, but unfortunately, there was no footage inside to show what they did. I thought that was kind of odd, because cameras were in there when we'd had our little popcorn fight. Somehow the cameras had disappeared. But I didn't need cameras. What else could they have been doing in there at two in the morning? More than that, I guess it was no big deal. The president was just like everybody else was. He probably needed some sex, too, and what better woman to get it from than Scorpio? She was always willing and able.

I kept watching the videos, only because I noticed some of the other things the president had been doing since he'd been here. He'd been definitely breaking the rules around here, and his phone usage was off the chain. I couldn't gripe about it because I was sure he'd had some important business to tend to on the side. Business that we didn't need to know about, but what I saw on the video next was, indeed, my business. I cocked my head back as I saw the president shove Chase against the wall. Fear was in her eyes as he choked the breath out of her. I couldn't believe what I was seeing, and I covered my mouth as saliva started to drip from it. I kept blinking to clear my watery eyes. My body started trembling, and when I saw her body hit the ground, I couldn't watch anymore. All I could think about was getting the fuck out of here. I wanted out, and I was so nervous and afraid that the president was going to kill all of us. But fuck everybody else. I was only going to save myself. I didn't have time to consult with anybody, and I feared that when I left this room, his ass would be somewhere lurking, watching and waiting for me. Tears ran from my eyes and cascaded down my face. I tiptoed out of the room, whimpering quietly as I made my way upstairs. The stairs squeaked loudly, but when I reached the top I felt relieved. It made me so nervous when I didn't see the president on the sofa. That was where he normally was at this time of the night; he was there when I had gone downstairs. I couldn't stop crying. My stomach hurt, and with every step toward the front door, I snapped my head from side-to-side, watching my surroundings. I couldn't wait to reach the door, and when I touched the knob, I turned it, pulled the door open and sprinted so fast that I wound up skidding down the driveway, after I fell and banged up my knees. The pain, however, didn't stop me. I got up, running as fast as I could. It was times like this that I wished I was athletic. I wished I could hop over fences . . . Lord, I wished I was about two or three pounds lighter so I could run just a little bit faster. I was moving, but it was as if the house was following me. I hadn't gotten far, until I decided to run to the next block over where Hell House was no longer in my view. My chest, however, burned. My legs throbbed so badly, and my arms were weak. I cried so hard that my vision was blurred. I saw bright headlights coming my way, and as I dove in somebody's yard to hide myself behind a bush, the car had passed. It was a white man driving, but as I tried to run after his car to catch him, he sped up and took off. I just had to keep on moving, until I reached a gas station or something. I needed to call somebody and tell them what the president had done. He was no good. He was dangerous. I hated that I'd voted for him, and what in the hell would a man like him do to this country? He would destroy it; maybe, that was his intentions. I couldn't stop thinking about the look in Chase's eyes, and even though I didn't like her, I never wanted something like that to happen to her. God . . . this was a mess! What had I gotten myself into—those were my thoughts as I kept on running. I had made some progress now, and as I reached a curvy, two-lane road that I knew had a gas station on it, I finally slowed down. I bent over, placing my hands on my knees and trying my best to catch my breath. The producers at Hell House could keep their damn money. I didn't want it nor did I need it. I would never go back to that house again, and I wasn't so sure if snitching on the president was the right thing to do. From where I came from, WE DIDN'T SNITCH! No, sir, not me. Then again, I stood up straight, thinking about how much a video like that could be worth. Somebody probably wanted it, and they would, most likely, pay me millions for it. I thought hard about what to do, and the more I'd thought about it, well . . . the last thing I would be considered was a fool!

Hi, Readers! Hope you enjoyed *Hell House Returns,* and the next book will conclude this series. Meanwhile, if you would like to read more about these characters, be sure to check out my novels that include them.

Thanks a million and don't forget to post a review.

Keith and Evelyn: *BFF's Series*

Roc: *Plus Size Diva: Who Ya Wit the Beginning (Full Figured 1,3,5)* and

Who Ya Wit the Finale

Scorpio and Mario: *Jaylin: A Naughty Aftermath (The Naughty Series)*

Jada: *How Can I Be Down?*

Chase: *Don't Even Go There*

Mr. President: *Black President: The World Will Never Be The Same*

Happy Reading!!

www.brendamhampton.com

CPSIA information can be obtained
at www.ICGtesting.com
Printed in the USA
LVOW13s1026120317

526915LV00009B/922/P